THE GREATEST FEAST

-Third Movie-

ERENS LUDIK

Erens Ludik

Dedication

First of all, I want to thank Abba Father God and His Son, Jesus Christ, for His goodness to me. Also, thanks to the precious Holy Spirit, the constant Helper in my heart and thought processes.

Thirdly, I want to thank both my parents, Hennie and Anita, who taught me positive lessons in life. As my father had passed away in 1994, my mother's constant help through thick and thin was and is still outstanding. Also, respect to my stepfather, John Hoskins, for his great wisdom and support over the years.

Fourthly, to my precious children Christian, Jessica and Christel. May you fulfil your destiny in God.

Lastly, to my 2 brothers, Jacques and Hein.
I am happy to have two great brothers, but I am also happy that I am the youngest. ☺

Acknowledgements

This is the third movie script out of the Trilogy series, and it's important to acknowledge that without the Trinity of God, all this would not be possible. All glory must go to the Father, The Son and the Holy Spirit, the Three in One !!!

As the idea unfolded and was put into writing, I have some important people to thank who played a pivotal role in helping me through my exciting journey in writing the storyline.

First of all, my mother, Anita Ludik-Hoskins, who helped me with the correct grammar. She was always there along the road, faithfully helping as the script developed.

Secondly, Dr Andrew McDonald. A very good friend with a great sense of humour. A lot of the funny scenes in the script have to do with his input. He was also instrumental in editing the script. A true friend!

Thirdly, Stella Heyns who helped polish this initial rough diamond of a script into an eternal shining bright diamond. Her talent speaks for itself, and she played an extremely important role bringing class to the script. I will be forever grateful for that!

About the Author

Erens Ludik, an entrepreneur with a wealth of business experience, has a passionate heart for God and His people. He is a great encourager who aims to help people find their true destiny on earth. He has written an Epic Trilogy about the End Times in a movie script format. It's full of romance, drama, action and unveiling of the End with great accuracy.

<u>Contact Erens Ludik</u>

Email: erensludik@yahoo.co.uk

Mobile : 00447802477830 (WhatsApp)

Opening Scene

(It's the year 535 BC. Daniel the prophet is standing on the bank of the great river, The Tigris. As he looked up there before him, he saw 2 men on both sides of the river. Then he looked over the waters, and he saw a man dressed in linen with a belt of fine gold around his waist. His body is like topaz, his face is like lightning, his eyes are like flaming torches, his arms and legs are like the gleam of burnished bronze, and his voice is like the sound of a multitude. He said with a loud voice:

"And from the time that the daily sacrifice is taken away, and the abomination of desolation is set up, there shall be one thousand two hundred and ninety days. Blessed is he who waits and comes to the one thousand three hundred and thirty-five days.")

Next scene

Cape Town

In the year 2040

(The same day that the Rapture took place. Hennie, from the last scene in "The Greatest Departure movie", is talking to Ingrid, the girl on Church Street opposite The Strand Beach. They continue their discussion of why they didn't make the Rapture.)

WOMAN ON THE STREET

So, you think we have missed the rapture because we were bad people?

MAN ON THE STREET

No, I think we have missed it because we didn't give our lives to Him.

WOMAN ON THE STREET

So, what do we do now?

MAN ON THE STREET

Well, the first thing is we need to give our lives to Him.

WOMAN ON THE STREET

How do we do it?

MAN ON THE STREET

Let's first go to the beach and pray and ask forgiveness.

WOMAN ON THE STREET

I think that is a good idea, and then we can submit our lives to Him together.

MAN ON THE STREET

Let's do it. Sorry I didn't ask your name.

INGRID

I am Ingrid. It's nice to meet you!

HENNIE

I am Hennie. The consummate pleasure is mine.

(They shake hands.)

(They both go on the beach and ask the Lord for forgiveness and submit their lives to Christ.)

INGRID

That felt good. It seems like we are in this together. I guess we might as well get to know each other. Tell me about yourself.

HENNIE

Well, money was my religion. Always hustling, always chasing that next million. And I was pretty good at it too! My goal was to be a billionaire before I reached the age of 30. And, of course, with the money came the lifestyle. I believed myself to be a regular James Bond. I even got an Aston Martin.

INGRID

Oh, I get it. Live fast, live fun. Life in the fast lane. That was my motto! I mean, as long as it was fun, light, no strings, no responsibilities.

I wasn't hurting anybody. I was a pretty good person. People liked me, and I was such an inspirational influencer to my followers. I thought that would be enough. But I guess we do need a Saviour.

HENNIE

I agree with you.

INGRID

Hey, you know what? I like you.

HENNIE

And I like you too. Shall we go for a drive around the mountain?

INGRID

Yeah, why not.

(Hennie and Ingrid are walking towards Hennie's Aston Martin. They get in the car and turn on the music.)

(The song plays "Higher Love" by Steve Winwood.)

Next Scene

(They arrive at a private beach behind Gordon's Bay Mountain. They park the car and go down the steps to the private beach. They discuss their feelings.)

HENNIE

Maybe we were meant to meet? Call it destiny, the divine intervention of God.

INGRID

I don't know if it is the situation or the divine intervention, but I feel strangely drawn to you. It's like I have known you all my life.

(They kiss each other.)

HENNIE

You know what?

INGRID

Tell me.

HENNIE

I don't know how much time we have left on this earth, but I think we should make it count as we have begun the countdown.

INGRID

What are you saying?

HENNIE

I think let's not waste time. Let's get married.

(Ingrid is blushing.)

INGRID

I can't believe I am saying this, but I think it's a marvellous idea!

(They kiss again and embrace with passion.)

HENNIE

I know a jewellery shop in Gordon's Bay. Let's go see if the owner is still there and if it is still open. He will have some rings we can choose from!

INGRID

You are serious, aren't you?

HENNIE

I have never been so serious in my life before. Let's go before they close.

INGRID

(Ingrid is standing still for a moment and thinking.) This feels right. And I feel right about this. (*Looking him in the eye.)* Yes, let's do it. Let's go. Together. (*They kiss each other.)*

(The song plays "James Dean" by Bonnie Tyler.)

Next Scene

(Hennie and Ingrid are driving off to RPS Diamonds. They arrive at the Jewellery shop. They are looking for a ring. They are speaking to Bob, the owner of the shop.)

BOB

How can I help you? You two look like you are in love. It's good to see people in love with everything that's happening around us.

HENNIE

Yes, we are. As a matter of fact, we are looking for a ring to get married to.

BOB

Well, you are at the right place. I have a jewellery designer who can design a ring for you.

HENNIE

That would be great. But first, I think my brand new fiancée should pick a diamond! Can you show us a few?

BOB

Sure, what type of cut are you after?

INGRID

I think a "princess" cut will be great.

HENNIE

That is a good choice. After all, you are a princess.

(Ingrid is blushing. I bet you say that to all the girls. *Everyone laughs.)*

BOB

Ok, guys, come here. Let me show you a few options.

(They choose the diamond and give it to the jewellery designer. Hennie also chooses a ring with a tanzanite stone. They are leaving the shop and going to Hennie's house in Gordan's Bay.)

Next Scene

(Hennie and Ingrid are sitting on the sofa. They are talking about their future together.)

INGRID

Soooo, we are really doing this, hey? (*Giggle.)* When do you think we should do it?

HENNIE

What about next weekend? The rings will be ready, and it gives us a few days to get everything sorted out.

INGRID

Unbelievable, so magical... Now I am really getting excited! Where do you think we should do it? Any place with specific meaning or significance for you..?

HENNIE

I have an idea. Let me keep it a secret for now.

(They are kissing.)

Next Scene

(It's the next weekend, Saturday night. Hennie and Ingrid are at a private beach at the back of Gordon's Bay. They are getting married. Only the 2 of them are there. Hennie looks at Ingrid in amazement. She looks so beautiful in the soft dusk air. She is dressed in a light and airy but simple white dress and bare feet. She has a flower crown of small white flowers braided into her long hair that moves with the soft summer breeze. Her best feature, though, is the broad smile on her lips and the loving gaze in her eyes.)

INGRID

Wow, this is an amazing spot. The view is incredible.

HENNIE

Indeed. The view in front of me, the vision beside me, and the future. All looks incredible. *(Smiling.)*

INGRID

(Blushing.)

Ok, only one question.

HENNIE

Fire away.

INGRID

Who is going to marry us?

HENNIE

God. *(Hennie is smiling.)*

INGRID

Well, that works for me.

(Hennie and Ingrid have a prayer together. They are asking God to marry them.)

(It's a beautiful sunset, and they are the only ones on the beach. They drive home.)

Next Scene

(Hennie and Ingrid are in bed sleeping. Hennie has a dream from God. He sees the return of Jesus with His saints. He sees them coming with white horses out of the clouds towards Jerusalem. He awakens... Ingrid also awakes, and they talk about the dream.)

INGRID

Well, Good Morning. "Husband"! (*In a sleepy voice.*) Wait, what's wrong? Why are you up so early? (*Sitting upright.*) Did I steal all the blankets? Oh no, did I snore? (*Horrified look.)*

HENNIE

No, my "Wife" nothing like that...! I had a dream. (*Smiling at her antics, but then gets serious.)* No, I had a dream.

INGRID

Ok, you're scaring me a little. Tell me about it.

HENNIE

I saw Jesus coming with the saints on white horses to earth.

INGRID

Wow, that sounds…quite amazing. What do you think it means?

HENNIE

I am not sure…Something inside me tells me that I need to pray and ask God to show me more. We are both new to this, but I feel it in my bones that God wants to tell us something…

INGRID

Yeah, from my rusty Sunday School memories, this sounds like something from Revelation – the last book in the Bible. Maybe we can see something there.
I guess it's worth a shot?

HENNIE

That's a great idea. Let's make breakfast, then get right into it.

(Ingrid gives Hennie a kiss, and they have breakfast together. After breakfast, they are sitting at the kitchen table with their Ipads reading Chapter 19 out of the book of Revelation. They talk to each other about it.)

INGRID

Whoah*! (her eyes grew big)* When do you think this will happen?

HENNIE

Very shortly, we could be weeks away, I think.

INGRID

What makes you say that?

HENNIE

I have a feeling, but we need to look more into the scripture to make sure.

Next Scene

(In La Rochelle, France, a married couple named Francois and Natalie are talking about God and giving their lives to Him.

The town of La Rochelle is almost empty. Only a few people are left after the Rapture.)

FRANCOIS

I can't believe we have missed the Rapture! You know, my family always told me about it. I had some very devoted Christians in my family. I always thought they were exaggerating or spinning old wives' tales…

NATALIE

Me too! I am shocked. My mother spoke a lot about the rapture before she died. Although we are Jewish, my parents were Messianic Jews – they accepted Jesus as the Messiah. They wanted the same for me, but I always thought there would be more time…I thought maybe one day, when I am older like them, maybe I will get 'there' and make a commitment.

FRANCOIS

Well, we have to figure out what we should do now.

NATALIE

What do you think? You are always the one that comes up with great ideas.

FRANCOIS

Well, I think we should repent and ask Him for a second chance. Everyone deserves a second chance.

NATALIE

Maybe. If I remember my family members' words and advice, I think we should pray, repent and ask Him for a second chance.

(Francois and Natalie are hugging each other. Tears flow from their eyes. They start praying together and gives their lives to Christ)

Next scene

(Francois and Natalie are back in Paris. They witness an incident where Jordan, from the New York taxi scene in the first movie, "The 4 Horses" of the Trilogy series, is stealing white running shoes from a Nike shop).

(He goes around the corner and quickly puts on the running shoes and runs further to a Rolex shop to steal Rolex watches. He is stopped by 2 policemen.)

POLICE OFFICER

Stop!

JORDAN

Don't touch me; I have a license to steal. MI6 told me to get all the Rolexes I could in the shop.

POLICE OFFICER

Right, you know we can track all people.

JORDAN

No, you can't. I was not that stupid. I didn't take that stupid Mark of the Beast.

(Jordan disappears and appears in front of Francois and Natalie.)

FRANCOIS

How did you get here? We saw the whole thing.

JORDAN

I have teleported.

FRANCOIS

Wow. Actually, there was this one guy in the Bible; I think his name was Philip - He teleported.

JORDAN

Gosh, say what now? In the Bible? The real Bible? Yeah right.

(*Incredulous eye-rolling.)*

And who was this Philip character you want me to believe teleported Star Trek-style...?

FRANCOIS

He was an evangelist in the Bible who appeared according to the Bible at a different location after preaching the gospel to an Ethiopian Eunuch.

JORDAN

Oh, you're being for real?? Legit like in Star Trek? Wow.

FRANCOIS

Correct. When was the first time that this happened to you?

JORDAN

Never before. I always wanted to do that. It happened as I was saying to the police officer that I hadn't taken the Mark of the Beast.

FRANCOIS

So, what's your plan now?

JORDAN

I don't know. Everyone I know is taken away.

FRANCOIS

Welcome to the party. You can join us.

JORDAN

Thanks, I don't know where you are going or what your plans are, but I guess in times like these, we need to stick together. Sounds like a plan!

FRANCOIS

This is Natalie, my wife.

JORDAN

Nice to meet you, Natalie.

NATALIE

Pleased to meet you, Jordan. You seem like an interesting person.

JORDAN

Thanks.

FRANCOIS

So, Jordan, you are welcome to come with us for a meal at our place. It's a nice area among the Champagne farms.

JORDAN

That will be awesome!

Next Scene

(They are driving to Francois and Natalie's place near the Champagne area. The sky is blue.)

FRANCOIS

Jordan, tell us a bit more about you.

JORDAN

I was a financial trader for a company in New York that trades on Wall Street, but as Shakespeare would say, "I lost the plot."

FRANCOIS

So, what happened to you?

JORDAN

You see, everything went well until I made a few bad calls…resulting in large trading losses for my employer. So, they fired me. I lost everything. I ended up on the street. It affected me so much that I lost my friends and family too. I pushed them away…Luckily one friend still believed in me and helped me move out of my environment. He helped me to start a new life in Paris.

Next Scene

(Gordon's Bay. Hennie and Ingrid are sitting in their house on the mountain overlooking the beach. They are discussing how he had made his money.)

INGRID

This house is awesome. It's funny – we shared so many deep significant things the last few days, but you never told me how you got this "James Bond Lifestyle", as you call it. (*Teasing.)* So, tell me, Hennie, how did you actually make your money?

HENNIE

Well, I did it with Real Estate and Hotel Apartments. I was focusing mainly on Gordon's Bay Area as I love the area and realised its potential.

INGRID

That's pretty perfect.

HENNIE

And why did you become a nurse?

INGRID

I have always loved people and felt compassion for people that are injured, and I wanted to help where I could.

(Hennie gives Ingrid a kiss, and they hug each other.)

HENNIE

So, where do you want to go on your honeymoon?

INGRID

(Giggles.) Ooooh, Husband! Honeymoon? That sounds amazing. But will we have time? More importantly, will we be able to travel..?

HENNIE

Let me worry about that…*(winking)*

INGRID

Well, then there's only one place – PARIS! The City of Love.

HENNIE

So, Paris it is. (*Hennie kisses Ingrid.)*

INGRID

But, seriously, how will we get there? There are hardly any planes flying anymore, plus with all of them, you need a chip in your body to pay for it, and we don't have it.

HENNIE

Praise God we haven't! Don't worry, I know an airline we can use.

INGRID

Which airline?

HENNIE

Saints 888 Airline. They also have rental cars available.

INGRID

Oh yeah – you're right! I remember now… that is the Christian airline, right? (*Pauses.)* But wait, wouldn't that mean that they are all gone with the Rapture?

HENNIE

My father worked for them. He told me before the Rapture that they had made provision for the people that's left behind that wanted to turn to God.

INGRID

How did they make provision?

HENNIE

They have employed believers and unbelievers. They had the hope that the unbelievers left behind would turn to Jesus.

INGRID

Wow, interesting. Your father was also part of the people that went with the Rapture?

HENNIE

Yes. If I only had listened to him.

INGRID

Yes, but at least you have listened now. And at least now we have met each other, and we are together.

HENNIE

That's true.

INGRID

So that's amazing that we can still use the Saints 888 Airline.

Next scene

(Hennie and Ingrid are at the Eiffel Tower in Paris. They are holding hands and enjoying the scenery. ***The song plays "Someone to You" by Banners.)***

HENNIE

You complete my life. It's like I found my missing puzzle piece…without knowing what it looked like, how to search for it or that it actually was what I was looking for until now. Now that the puzzle piece is in, I can see the complete picture.

INGRID

Oh, my love, I feel the same!

(They kiss each other.)

HENNIE

Did you always want to come here to Eiffel Tower in Paris?

INGRID

Yes, my dream is fulfilled now, and I have the best husband; life can't get better than this.

HENNIE

Oh yes! There is one more thing.

INGRID

What's that?

HENNIE

I want to take you for a drive around the Champagne area, and then we can see the countryside a bit.

INGRID

Oh gosh! That will be great!

HENNIE

Yeah, let's go.

INGRID

Wow, this is only getting better!

Next Scene

(Hennie and Ingrid are driving to the Champagne area. At the same time, Francois and Natalie are driving back with Jordan from their house to Paris. A biker is on his Harley Davidson. He is speeding very fast. He overtakes Hennie and Ingrid. As he overtakes, he goes too far on the other side and crashes into Francois and Natalie's car.
His bike goes over the car, and he falls into the bushes. He is still alive but is breathing badly. Francois stops his car. Hennie and Ingrid also stop.)

FRANCOIS

Sir, are you ok?

(The biker finds it hard to say anything. Meanwhile, Hennie and Ingrid are on the scene. Hennie introduces everybody to Francois.)

HENNIE

Good afternoon Sir. I am Hennie, and this is my wife, Ingrid. She is a nurse. Maybe it's a good idea that she takes care of him while we try to get hold of the Emergency services.

FRANCOIS

That's a bright idea. Let me phone the ambulance.

(Meanwhile, the biker is struck by a Bright Light. Jesus appears to him.)

JESUS

Jean, it's time to turn your life to me. I need you for a special mission. The people around you are part of your team. I have brought the whole group together for a special task before I return with My Bride.
You should call your mission "The Last Call" because this is "My last call" to whoever is left behind on earth to turn to Me. I am the

Alpha and the Omega. I am bringing one more woman to the team who is from Damascus, Syria, and then the group is complete.

(Jesus disappears.)

(While Ingrid is attending to The Biker and Francois is calling the Emergency Services, Natalie and Jordan get on the scene too. They are introducing each other to Hennie.)

NATALIE

Hey, I am Natalie.

HENNIE

Hello Natalie. I am Hennie. Are you ok?

NATALIE

Yes, I am fine. This is Jordan.

HENNIE

Nice to meet you, Jordan.

JORDAN

Same to you. It feels so strange meeting you all.

NATALIE

Yes, it's refreshing to meet some good people. It feels like all the good people have left the earth.

HENNIE

That's very close to the truth. We need to see what we can do now. Hopefully, we still have a part to play.
(A girl originally from Damascus, Syria, called Katia, is stopping at the scene of the accident and asks if she can help. Jordan is meeting her.)

KATIA

Good day. Oh, my goodness, what happened here? Is anybody hurt? I am a trained First Aider. I can help!

JORDAN

Good day Madame. It's kind of you to stop. We have called the ambulance, and we have a nurse that is attending to the man.

KATIA

Oh, ok – that's good to hear. But maybe I can at least assist until help arrives.

JORDAN

No problem. I am sure you can.

HENNIE

Well, my wife is attending to the guy. You are welcome to speak to her.

KATIA

Thanks.

(Katia is talking to Ingrid. She is helping her. In the meantime, Hennie and Francois are getting to know each other. They exchange numbers.)

Next scene

(Jean Claude, the biker, is now released from the hospital. He is at his mansion in Versailles with the whole group. He is a billionaire. He is married to Abigail, and they have a daughter called Jasmine, who is 10 years old. Abigail's father owns a jet oil company in Baghdad. He becomes a Christian after that night, and he starts supplying Saints 888 Airline with Jet Oil.)

(The whole group are sitting around a bonfire at Jean Claude's house. Hennie is asking Jean about the background of the mansion.)

HENNIE

You know, Jean, I do real estate for a living, but I have never seen a place like this before. Can you tell us more about this mansion?

JEAN CLAUDE

Sure. Well, it actually has an interesting story – it was built on the same land as the Versailles Palace. Back then, the land was sold to an aristocratic family, who lived in it for a few generations. I was able to acquire it about 20 years ago. Through the years, I have made some changes and renovated it to what you see now.

HENNIE

You did an amazing job. It is quite exquisite!

JEAN CLAUDE

Thank you.

FRANCOIS

So, Jean, hope you feel better now after the accident. We are thankful that we had arrived when we did and that we could help, but inviting us here is very generous of you and not at all necessary. We are just grateful that we were at the right place, at the right time!

JEAN CLAUDE

I am much better, thanks. But, Francois, you have no idea how right you are about the timing…Something happened after the accident – there at the very scene. That's why I invited all of you tonight…

NATALIE

Now, you have got us very interested.

INGRID

Yes, please tell us more. Now, you've got me worried. We really just tried to help – did we do something wrong at the scene?

JEAN CLAUDE

No, no, no, dear Ingrid. You and Katia were amazing – like two angels. No, it was something else…something extraordinary… Jesus appeared to me while I was lying there. It was like a bright light was shining on me…

KATIA

Really??? What did He say?

JEAN CLAUDE

He told me that He had called me for a special mission, but not only me.
All of us.
(There is silence in the room.)

HENNIE

(Swallowing loudly.) I suspected that there was a reason why we were still here…. (*Asking softly)* What else did He say? Did He tell you what our mission was?

JEAN CLAUDE

Yes, we should try and win as many souls for Christ. He told me we should call our mission "The Last Call".

HENNIE

It sounds like the last call to the passengers at an airport to go on the plane for boarding.

JEAN CLAUDE

Exactly.

(Jean Claude's wife Abigail and their daughter Jasmine are coming to join the group outside.)

JEAN CLAUDE

We have lots to discuss, but I first want to introduce you to my lovely wife, Abigail and our daughter Jasmine. Well, guys, here comes my beautiful wife Abigail and our daughter Jasmine.

(They all say hello to her.)

ABIGAIL

Nice to meet you all.

JEAN CLAUDE

Abigail's father, Ali, will join us a bit later. He is just chasing up some urgent work matters. He is in charge of one of the largest Jet Oil companies in the world, situated in Baghdad, so the two-hour time difference is always something to consider.

HENNIE

That sounds so interesting.

FRANCIOS

Now, I get it! Your daughter is Jasmine – as in Princess Jasmine – as in Aladdin!
Aladdin / Baghdad – now I get it! (*Everyone is smiling.)*

JEAN CLAUDE

Mmmmmm...Not just a pretty face, ey! Got that all figured out! (*Jean Claude winks at Francois.)*

FRANCOIS

Speaking of…there's something else I want to figure out, too… humour me?

JEAN CLAUDE

Shoot.

FRANCOIS

If I am not mistaken, The Palace of Versailles was built during the reign of Louis XIV?

JEAN CLAUDE

Correct. He is also called Louis the Great or the Sun King.

FRANCOIS

And he was the king that revoked the Edict of Nantes, right?

JEAN CLAUDE

Correct again.

INGRID

Aaaah, yes! We learned of that in our history classes in school. Isn't that how some French Huguenots ended up in South Africa? Because they had to flee from France..? My forefathers are from France. Bonjour!! (*Everyone smiles at the greeting and little curtsy.)*

KATIA

Why are they called French Huguenots?

FRANCIOS

Because they were part of the protestant movement. King Louis XIV was a Catholic king. That's why he revoked the Edict of Nantes, which gave protection to the protestants in the time of the Protestant movement.

KATIA

Oh, I see. The Christians from Syria are Orthodox. Sorry, I am not familiar with that. When did the protestant movement start?

HENNIE

It started with Martin Luther on Reformation Day, the 31st of October 1517, when he nailed The 95 Theses on the door of the All Saints Church in Wittenberg, Germany.

KATIA

I see.

NATALIE

Katia, can you tell us a bit about you? How did you end up here?

KATIA

Well, I am from Damascus. I moved here with my parents when the war in the Middle East became intense. They were devoted Christians, so they were Raptured…I was still rebellious, I thought there would be lots of time still to go, so I hadn't given my life to Christ at that time. I, too, had a spiritual experience after the Rapture.

NATALIE

I can't wait to hear your story.

KATIA

So, I went into the Notre Dame Cathedral after the Rapture to find comfort. I saw one of the paintings of Maria, the mother of Jesus. Suddenly, I saw blood coming out of her eyes. I tried to ask people there about it, but no one saw what I saw.

INGRID

What did you do then?

KATIA

I knelt down on the nearest church pew and gave my life to Christ.

INGRID

That's an amazing story.

KATIA

Yeah, I think I have found amazing grace by meeting you guys too.

NATALIE

We feel the same. We are blessed to meet each other. Jean is right. God must have put each one of us together for His purpose.

JEAN CLAUDE

What about you, Jordan? Have you given your life to Christ?

JORDAN

I haven't, but now I would like to.

JEAN CLAUDE

That's brilliant. We will pray for you tonight. I have some good news too. Obviously, after the accident, I did give my life to Christ, and so did Abigail and Jasmine. When her father comes soon, he also wants to give his life. So that means all of us will be saved. Amen.

(They all sit and enjoy the warmth of the bonfire. Ali arrives, and the group pray for Jordan and Ali. They both give their lives to Christ.)

(The song plays: My Jesus, My Saviour (Darlene Zschech).

Next scene

(Jean Claude has invited the whole group for dinner at his Champagne farm. There are 2 waitresses serving them. One is called Kasia, who is from Poland originally, and the other one is Kim, who is from Edinburgh, Scotland. The group arrives at the vineyard.)

JEAN CLAUDE

Morning girls! I have a group of new friends here and lots to tell you!!

KASIA AND KIM

Morning boss!

JEAN CLAUDE

I am not your boss anymore. I call you my friends now. (*Jean Claude is smiling.)*

(The girls are confused.)

JEAN CLAUDE

Yeah, Jesus has changed my life. I need to tell you the whole story.

KASIA

That sounds very interesting.

(*The two girls are looking at him with amazement.)*

KIM

Yes, we can't wait to hear.

JEAN CLAUDE

Ok, get a table ready for my friends, then sit down and let me tell you.

(The girls are preparing the table and sit down. Jean is telling them the whole story. They are taken aback. Jordan is sitting next to Katia. Immediately Jean notices the exchanged looks and connection between Jordan & Katia.)

JEAN CLAUDE

I see we have two lovebirds here. (*Jean Claude is smiling, and everyone looks at Jordan and Katia. Katia is blushing.)*

FRANCOIS

This is what happens in France. (*The romance kicks off very quickly. Francois gives Jordan a wink.)*

(The food arrives with Champagne, and everyone enjoys the lunch. It's sunset and time to go. They drive back.)

Next scene

(Jean Claude is at his home speaking to his wife Abigail about the future.)

ABIGAIL

Jean, how long do you think we have left before Jesus will return with His Bride?

JEAN CLAUDE

I think we are talking about 2-3 weeks.

ABIGAIL

How come so short a time?

JEAN CLAUDE

I have read a few scriptures in the Bible concerning this time. It makes it crystal clear to me.

ABIGAIL

Could you share that with me?

JEAN CLAUDE

Of course, honey. Let me read it for you. Look at this passage in the Bible.

(Jean Claude is showing Daniel 12:11 on his iPad to Abigail.)

11 "And from the time that the daily sacrifice is taken away, and the abomination of desolation is set up, there shall be one thousand two hundred and ninety days."

ABIGAIL

What are that 1290 days about?

JEAN CLAUDE

It is about the number of days from when Syria took Jerusalem at the start of the Great Tribulation till Jesus comes back with His Bride.

ABIGAIL

How did you get to that conclusion?

JEAN CLAUDE

It is because The Great Tribulation was 1260 days. Remember the 2 witnesses?

ABIGAIL

Of course. Who would forget them?

JEAN CLAUDE

In Revelation 11:3, it says: “And I will give power to my two witnesses, and they will prophesy one thousand two hundred and sixty days, clothed in sackcloth.”

ABIGAIL

I see what you are getting at. So, on the day they died, the 1260 days stopped?

JEAN CLAUDE

You are so smart. So, after the two witnesses died, they were resurrected after 3 and a half days and shortly after that, the Rapture took place.

ABIGAIL

So, now I get why you said 2-3 weeks because then the 1290 days will be completed.

JEAN CLAUDE

You got it. We are fast learners. (*They both smile. Jean Claude gives Abigail a kiss)*

Next Scene

(Francois and Natalie are at their home discussing the events of the last couple of days.)

NATALIE

What an interesting few days we had.

FRANCOIS

You can say that again.

NATALIE

I like everyone in our new special group. (*Natalie is smiling.)*

FRANCOIS

We are all so different, but still, we fit in so well. Look at Katia; she is Syrian, and you are Jewish. The whole war started in Jerusalem, and it was because of an attack from the Syrian government.

NATALIE

Yes, I am so looking forward to our next meeting with the group. I would like to know what the strategy is for us.

FRANCOIS

Me too. I will call Jean tomorrow to see when we are meeting up again.

Next Scene

(It's in the evening. Jean, Claud and Abigail go to bed. Jesus wakes Jean up and speaks to him.)

JESUS

Jean, I am here to give you a bit more understanding of what I want you and the group to do. As you know, the world is in turmoil, and the time is very close for me to return with My bride. I want you and the team to go to specific places in the world where I have people to be called to Me but are in difficult situations because of the Antichrist and his armies.
You have only a few days to do this before I display My wrath on this earth. My wrath comes because people don't want to receive My Grace anymore. I will show you the specific areas in the morning when you spend time with Me.
Be strong, and your team will do well.

(Jesus disappears.)

Next scene

(It's night time. The moon is bright. Jordan is walking in the park in Paris, holding hands with Katia. They are speaking about their relationship and about marriage.)

(The song plays "I think we're alone now " by Tiffany.)

JORDAN

Katia, you know I like you. I have been speaking to Hennie and Ingrid. They have known each other for a week before they got married. They decided to get married because of the short time before Jesus is set to return. I was thinking about us.

KATIA

What have you been thinking about us, Jordan? (*Katia is smiling.)*

JORDAN

Well, I was thinking could we do the same? (*Jordan is smiling.)*

KATIA

You know what? The world is so crazy, and I am sure I will not find a person like you again. So, I think let's go for it. (*Katia is blushing.)* But you better ask me in a very romantic way.

JORDAN

Don't worry. I have it all sorted. I promise you. It's a surprise.

(Jordan kisses Katia.)

Next scene

(Hennie and Ingrid are in their place in Paris. They are talking about the events of the past few days.)

HENNIE

Ingrid, it looks like we haven't come here just because of the Eiffel tower. It seems God had a bigger reason for bringing us here.

INGRID

Yeah, God has us here for His great plan.

HENNIE

Yeah, it seems so.

INGRID

I see God works with a team of people, and we are all part of a team.

HENNIE

Yeah, it's actually exciting!

INGRID

You did mention before that the time is very short, so every day counts.

HENNIE

On that note, let's go to bed. We are actually on honeymoon, if I remember correctly. (*Hennie is smiling. They kiss and go to bed.)*

Next scene

(It's the next day. Jean is calling everyone to meet up at his place. The group is gathering at Jean's place.)

JEAN CLAUDE

So, gang, we are here to talk about our mission. Let's make it short, for we haven't got time to waste.

FRANCOIS

I agree. Tell us what's next as we are ready as can be.

JEAN CLAUDE

Jesus was speaking with me of some places we have to go to save some people.

HENNIE

We are all ears.

JEAN CLAUDE

He was talking about Baghdad, Bolivia, Kazakhstan and Syria.

FRANCOIS

Wow, that's very specific.

JEAN CLAUDE

Yes indeed. I want you guys to pray about it. We need to cover all the places, which means a team of two assigned to each location.

KATIA

But Syria is such a dangerous place right now.

JEAN CLAUDE

Yes, for sure, but remember when God send you somewhere, He knows what He is doing.

NATALIE

I agree. Let's pray tonight, each one at home and see what the Lord reveals to us.

JEAN CLAUDE

A very good idea, Natalie. When you guys leave, I want you, Jordan and Katia to stay behind. I have something to tell you.

(Jordan and Katia are looking at each other puzzled.)

JEAN CLAUDE

Don't worry, you two, it's something good. (*Jean Claude is smiling.)*

(The group is leaving. Jordan and Katia are sitting next to Jean Claude.)

JEAN CLAUDE

I had a dream about you two last night. (*Jean Claude is smiling.)*

KATIA

What was the dream about? (*Katia is blushing.)*

JEAN CLAUDE

I saw you two getting married on my Champagne farm.

(Silence in the room.)

(The song plays "Nothing's Gonna Stop Us Now" by Starship.)

JEAN CLAUDE

You two are silent. (*Jean Claude smiles.)*

JORDAN

You put us on the spot. (*Jordan smiles***.** *Katia eases the atmosphere.)*

KATIA

You couldn't be more right. Jordan and I have discussed this before.

JEAN CLAUDE

God is never wrong, I guess. (*Jean Claude smiles and winks at them.)*

JORDAN

I guess not. *(Jordan whispers to Jean in his ear.)* We still need to get engaged first, and I have been planning it.

JEAN CLAUDE

Well then, you two lovebirds, do what you need to do. My Champagne farm is ready as can be for your wedding. (*Jordan and Katia hug Jean Claude and go.)*

Next scene

(Jordan and Katia are at the Eiffel Tower. Jordan is going on bended knee and ask Katia to marry him.)
(The song plays "Marry you" by Bruno Mars.)

JORDAN

Will you marry me?

KATIA

Of course.

(He puts the ring on her finger. She hugs and kisses him.)

(A woman from India, Deepika and her daughter Crystal are standing next to Jordan and Katia. She greets them and says congratulations to both of them.)

DEEPIKA

You two look so happy together. (*Congratulations.)*

KATIA

Oh, thank you very much.

JORDAN

You have a lovely daughter. What's her name?

DEEPIKA

Her name is Crystal.

KATIA

That's a beautiful name.

CRYSTAL

Thank you. (*Crystal is blushing.)*

JORDAN

Well, if you two are free, you are welcome to join us in a few days for the wedding.

KATIA

Yeah, that's a great idea.

DEEPIKA

We feel so honoured, and it will be a great pleasure too.

JORDAN

Perfect.

(They exchange numbers and say goodbye.)

Next scene

(It's the wedding day. The whole groups are there, plus Deepika and Crystal. Katia and Kim are Bridesmaids at the wedding.)

(The song plays "My heart will go on" by Celine Dion.)

(Jean Claude gives a speech at the wedding, and he gives Jordan a Rolex watch for his wedding and a blue diamond necklace for Katia.)

JEAN CLAUDE

Great to have all of you guys here. Give a huge hand to our newly married couple.

(Everyone is giving a huge standing ovation to Jordan and Katia. They enjoy their meal.)

Next scene

(It's evening, and Jordan and Katia go to bed. Katia has a dream about Jesus and His saints coming back on white horses. She awakes and wakes Jordan up.)

JORDAN

What is it, my love?

KATIA

I just had a dream.

JORDAN

Tell me.

KATIA

I saw Jesus with the saints coming with white horses through the clouds.

JORDAN

That's a great dream. You must tell the group about that.

KATIA

Yeah, definitely.

(It's the same night. Natalie also gets a dream. She dreams about the Hanukkah Feast. She sees the whole group and the saints together with Jesus and celebrating the Hanukkah Feast in Jerusalem. She recognises her parents too.)

(She suddenly wakes up. She decides to keep the dream to herself for the moment.)

Next scene

(The whole group gathers at Jean Claude's house. They have a good discussion about the future.)

JEAN CLAUDE

Hope you guys are all well. Does anyone have anything to share?

KATIA

Yes, I had a dream of Christ returning with His saints to earth on white horses.

HENNIE

That's amazing! I had the same dream before we came to France.

JEAN CLAUDE

Very interesting. That confirms that we are on the right track. Who else had any dreams too?

NATALIE

Me too. I, too, have dreamt. I dreamt about the Hanukkah Feast. We were all there.
I even saw my parents there.

JEAN CLAUDE

Now we are talking. Looks like the puzzles are coming together. Does anyone else have something to share? (*Jean Claude is looking at Jordan and smiles.)*

JORDAN

Well, I have been praying about the places you have mentioned where Jesus wants to send us.

JEAN CLAUDE

Brilliant. What do you sense?

JORDAN

I feel Katia and I have a mission to fulfil in Syria. It makes sense, as she is also from Syria originally.

JEAN CLAUDE

It sounds right to me. What about you, Francois?

FRANCOIS

I have also been praying about it. I feel me and Natalie are going to be sent to Bolivia.

JEAN CLAUDE

Why do you feel so?

FRANCOIS

When you mentioned Bolivia last time, I felt it resonate within my heart. I have an old-time friend there who was a Christian and was taken up with the Rapture, but his father is still there. I spoke with him a few days back. He also wants to give his life to Christ-like his son did. Then besides that, I was always interested in the place where the revolutionary Ernesto Che Guevara died. I think he missed the point of truth between humanism and choosing Jesus.

JEAN CLAUDE

I think you are correct. For me, it's obvious that Baghdad is my destiny as my wife and father-in-law are from there.

HENNIE

So, that means one thing, Ingrid and I are going to be sent to Kazakhstan?
(Hennie is smiling.)

JEAN CLAUDE

Well, figured out. (*Jean Claude smiles back.)*

Next scene

(Each couple is back at their homes and discussing the places they are going. Natalie is speaking to Francois.)

FRANCOIS

You never told me about your dream.

NATALIE

Yes, because I never had a spiritual dream like that before. I wanted to ponder about it before sharing it with you.

FRANCOIS

It was a very profound dream, but do you know what?

NATALIE

Tell me.

FRANCOIS

I am not surprised that God gave you that dream.

NATALIE

Why do you say that?

FRANCOIS

Because your name means Christmas, and Jesus was conceived in December.

NATALIE

That's interesting. I always thought He was born on Christmas Day.

FRANCOIS

I have looked it up. Jesus was conceived on the 8th of December. That's why the Catholics celebrate the feast of the Immaculate Conception on that day. On the Hebrew Calendar, Jesus was conceived on the 24th of Kislev.

NATALIE

The day before the Hanukkah feast starts.

FRANCOIS

Correct. You see, God gave me a Jewish wife for a reason. (*Francois is smiling.)*

NATALIE

Oh yeah, for what reason? (*Natalie is smiling.)*

FRANCOIS

Because He knows I like the look of you. (*Francois is smiling.)*

NATALIE

Hahahaha! Cutie. You know how to turn on the charm, don't you! (*They both giggle.)* Now, tell me the real reason?

FRANCOIS

So that I can tell you about the real meaning of Hanukkah. (*Francois is smiling.)*

NATALIE

You are such a charmer. Tell me more.

FRANCOIS

Ok, I will tell you. *(Francois gives Natalie a kiss.)*
All the Jews know the Hanukkah Feast, but it was only the Jews that accepted Jesus as their Messiah that understood that the Hanukkah

Feast is pointing to Christ. The middle candle represents Christ, which lights the other 8 candles. Jesus is the Light of the world.

NATALIE

That makes sense. I am so glad I gave my life to the Messiah.

FRANCOIS

Me too. (*Francois and Natalie are giving each other a hug.)*

Next scene

(Jordan and Katia are speaking about Syria.)

KATIA

I wonder why Jesus wants to send us to Syria?

JORDAN

Remember the vision you had in the Notre Dame Cathedral?

KATIA

Yes, very well. It changed my life.

JORDAN

I believe God gave you that vision not only to save you but to save others in your country that would receive Christ.

KATIA

Yes, but I am afraid of that place.

JORDAN

Don't worry; that's why Jesus gave you to me. I will be with you.

(Katia gives Jordan a hug and a kiss.)

KATIA

How do you think we are going to get there?

JORDAN

I have a strong feeling we will be teleported.

KATIA

Whaaat? Teleported? (*Katia is looking at Jordan with an incredible facial expression. Then starts smiling.)*

JORDAN

(Jordan is smiling too). Of course, My love. Remember I told you the story of what happened to me in Paris when the police chased me..?

KATIA

Yeah, I remember. So, do you think that was a sign that we would be travelling that way?

JORDAN

Yes, I do.

KATIA

Well, Jordan, I trust you. I wouldn't have married you if I didn't. (*Katia is smiling and gives Jordan a kiss.)*

Next scene

(Hennie and Ingrid are talking about Kazakhstan.)

INGRID

Don't you think it's a strange thing that Jesus wants to send us to Kazakhstan?

HENNIE

A bit. I mean, you don't know anything about Kazakhstan – do you?

INGRID

Nope.

HENNIE

Me neither. Luckily, we serve The One that created Kazakhstan and the people that live there. He is in control and always knows what He is doing.

INGRID

Yes, you are right.

(*Ingrid is putting her head on Hennie's chest.)*

Your heart is beating fast.

HENNIE

There must be two reasons for that.

INGRID

Oh yeah? What could that be? (*Ingrid is smiling.)*

HENNIE

First of all, my beloved is next to me.

INGRID

Oh, you are a Romantic now, mmmm?

HENNIE

Always been. (*Hennie is smiling.)*

INGRID

What is the second reason?

HENNIE

The second reason is our mission to Kazakhstan. It must be important if God highlighted that.

INGRID

Yes. Shall we book flight tickets via Saints 888 Airline?

HENNIE

Yes, but not only seats. I feel we should book a whole plane.

INGRID

What makes you think like that?

HENNIE

I have a feeling that God wants us to bring a whole plane full of people from Kazakhstan to Paris.

INGRID

Where are they going to stay? Also, how are we going to pay for hiring a whole plane?

HENNIE

God has already made provision.

INGRID

Do you mean through Jean Claude?

HENNIE

Exactly. Now is the time he will use all that money for a great eternal purpose.

INGRID

Wow, I know what you mean.

Next scene

(Jean Claude is sitting in his living room with Abigail, Ali and Jasmine.)

JEAN CLAUDE

So, how are you all feeling about our mission to Baghdad?

ALI

I am assured that God is going to do something great there.

JEAN CLAUDE

Yes, for sure, it's an important place.

ABIGAIL

I don't think it is a coincidence that we need to go to Baghdad.

JEAN CLAUDE

Why do you say so, Abigail?

ABIGAIL

That story of Aladdin comes into play.

JEAN CLAUDE

Why?

ABIGAIL

Because it makes perfect sense. Remember, good always overcome evil.

ALI

You are right. Aladdin found his princess, and they eventually won the day.

JEAN CLAUDE

That's why we called our daughter Jasmine. We believe in the good, although we didn't figure out the truth before the time. We won't make that mistake again.

ABIGAIL

You are right. Now we have the opportunity to save as many people as we can from our home country.

ALI

Yes, I can use my company to supply as much jet fuel as we need to fly the Saints 888 planes.

JEAN CLAUDE

That's brilliant.

ALI

My son-in-law, now we can work together to accomplish God's purpose.

(They give each other a hug.)

Next Scene

(Hennie is phoning Jean Claude. The phone is ringing...Jean Claude picks up the phone.)

JEAN CLAUDE

Hello, Hennie, my brother.

HENNIE

Hello Jean.

JEAN CLAUDE

What's up?

HENNIE

It's all good. I want to discuss something with you.

JEAN CLAUDE

No problem. Tell me.

HENNIE

Ingrid and I were discussing our trip to Kazakhstan.

JEAN CLAUDE

Ok, I am listening.

HENNIE

I reckon we have a good opportunity here… I think we can bring a whole plane full of new believers back from Kazakhstan.

JEAN CLAUDE

That's what I want to hear! And we can easily accommodate them.

HENNIE

That's what I told Natalie.

JEAN CLAUDE

Well, you are spot on. Ok, let's all meet up tomorrow for a final time before we all set off on our missions.

HENNIE

Ok, good.

JEAN CLAUDE

Have a good night.

HENNIE

You to Jean!

Next Scene

(The group are at Jean Claude's place for a final gathering before they set on their journeys to each one's destination. They have a shared meal in the living room. They are sitting around a 12-seated table and discussing the missions ahead.)

JEAN CLAUDE

Welcome, everyone!

FRANCOIS

Welcome to you, Jean Claude. Thanks for the feast here. The food looks delicious!

JEAN CLAUDE

Glad to have you all here. Bon Appetit! (Translation: "Enjoy your meal!")

KATIA

I must say something that I have loved about France since I left Syria is the food!
Especially here in La Paris.

JEAN CLAUDE

Why do you think Remy, the Ratatouille chef, is from France? (*Jean Claude is laughing.)*

KATIA

Ah, you are talking about the Ratatouille movie. (*She is smiling.)*

JEAN CLAUDE

You got it! Since you are so sharp, let's start with you and Jordan first. Are you guys ready for your mission?

JORDAN

Ready as can be! Katia and I have discussed her revelation at the Notre Dame Cathedral.
I believe God gave her that vision not only to save her but to go and save others in Syria before the return of Christ.

FRANCOIS

That sound's brilliant. You know that the Notre Dame Cathedral is such a magical and significant place. There is something about it.

JEAN CLAUDE

Yeah, did you know that the Cathedral was used as a halfway stop for saints on their pilgrim journey from the United Kingdom to Rome? It was dedicated to Mary, Jesus's mother.

KATIA

That explains why I had a vision of Mary's tears of blood coming out of her eyes.

FRANCOIS

Yeah, another interesting fact is that it is no coincidence that Charlemagne's statue is outside the Church.

HENNIE

Why?

FRANCOIS

He ruled during a very important time in history.
He was the first Holy Roman Emperor. He was coronated on Christmas Day, 800 AD, at the Old St. Peter Basilica in Rome.

NATALIE

That explains my name again, Christmas. (*Natalie is smiling.)*

JEAN CLAUDE

On that note, are you two ready for your journey?

FRANCOIS

Absolutely. We need a private jet. As we mentioned before we want to visit my friend's father. He is an ex- general in the military of Bolivia.

JEAN CLAUDE

That's a brave move on the chess board.

FRANCOIS

Indeed, it is. As you probably know, the Spanish have deep roots in South America. Apparently, it was in a chess game that Queen Isabelle of Castile helped King Ferdinand to win the game, and that put him in a good mood, and he decided to support Christopher Columbus on his journey to the New World.

JEAN CLAUDE

Well, you two also have an important mission in the heart of South America to save an ex-general for Christ before the new upcoming reign of Him on earth. Every soul counts!

FRANCOIS

I know. It's an honour.

JEAN CLAUDE

For sure, it is.
Hennie, you have mentioned that you need an empty plane. I have already organised with Saints 888 Airline a double-decker Airbus for your trip to Kazakhstan.

HENNIE

That's brilliant. Thank you very much, Jean!

JEAN CLAUDE

You are welcome. So, I think everyone is organised. We will meet up in a few days' time again once everyone is back. We haven't got a lot of time, so we will seize the day.

*(The song plays **Danger Zone by Kenny Loggins**.)*

Next scenes

(François and Natalie fly to La Paz, Bolivia with a Saints 888 Air superjet.

Jean Claude, Abigail, Jasmine and Ali are also flying in a Saints 888 Air superjet to Baghdad, Iraq.

Hennie and Ingrid are in a Saints 888 Airbus flying to Astana, Kazakhstan.

Jordan and Katia are teleported to Damascus, Syria. They walk in the street called "Straight Street, where Paul the apostle received his sight back after he was struck blind on the road to Damascus.)

Next scene

Francois and Natalie arrive at El Alto International Airport, La Paz, Bolivia. They are greeted by Diego Castillo, an ex-general in the military.

DIEGO CASTILLO

Hello, my dear friend Francois! I am so glad to see you. (*He gives Francois a hug.)*

FRANCOIS

Nice to see you again, Diego. This is my wife, Natalie.

DIEGO

Wow, she is lovely. Only the best for my dearest Francois. He gives her a kiss on her cheek.

NATALIE

Thank you. Glad to meet you!

DIEGO

Ok, let me take you to my place. We have some important things to discuss.

FRANCOIS

Yes, indeed, we have.

(They drive to Diego's house in Santa Cruz de la Sierra.)

Next scene

(Jean Claude and his family have arrived in Baghdad. They are in the house of an old friend, Rania, in Baghdad.)

ABIGAIL

Rania, I am so happy to see you.

RANIA

Me too, Abigail. (*Rania is crying.)* You know, since my dad was taken up with the Rapture, I couldn't stop crying. *(Tears are rolling down Rania's cheeks. Abigail hug her.)*

ABIGAIL

You know I have given my life to Christ. What about you, Rania?

RANIA

I want to.

ABIGAIL

So, let's do it. I will pray with you.
(Abigail is praying with Rania, and Rania gives her life to Christ.)

Next scene

(Hennie and Ingrid are at a school in Astana, Kazakhstan. Romy is the Head Teacher. There are many children. Hennie is speaking to Romy.)

HENNIE

Nice to meet you, Romy. My name is Hennie, and this is Ingrid, my wife. (*They shake hands.)*

ROMY

It's my honour to meet you. How can I help you?

HENNIE

Well, we are new Christians. We feel the Lord has called us here to reach out to people and bring them to safety in these troubled times.

ROMY

That's very kind of you. My wife, Anna, was also a Christian, but she was taken up with the Rapture, and I was left behind. Since then, I also have been giving my life to the Lord and speaking to my students about it. I was praying for help, and here you are.

INGRID

Wow. We are so glad to be here to help.

HENNIE

Yes, we have actually organised a plane so that we can bring people to a safe place in France.

ROMY

That's so awesome because we live in total fear here. The whole city is in an uproar, and there are killings day by day.

HENNIE

It seems we are in the right place at the right time.

ROMY

You can say that again.

Next Scene

(Jordan and Katia meet 69 people in an Armenian Orthodox Church in "Straight Street", Damascus. They form a prayer group and do outreach on the street to unbelievers. Katia is speaking to a lady, Maria, in the Church.)

KATIA

Hello, please to meet you. My name is Katia.

MARIA

Nice to meet you, Katia. I am Maria.

KATIA

If I may ask, who are all these people in here?

MARIA

They are family and friends of mine. We were all left behind when our families were taken away with the Rapture. We then gave our lives to Christ and have started to gather here together.

KATIA

That's amazing!

MARIA

Yes, this place is very significant in Christianity. The apostle Paul came to this street in AD 33 to be prayed for by Ananias, a disciple of Jesus Christ, so that he would receive his sight back and be converted to Christianity.

(Jordan appears on the scene.)

KATIA

Maria, this is Jordan. We just got married last week. We met in Paris.

MARIA

Wow, congratulations. You are a beautiful couple.

JORDAN

Thank you, Maria. (*They shake hands.)*

Next Scene

(Francois and Natalie are at Diego's house in Santa Cruz de la Sierra.)

FRANCOIS

So, Diego, do you live here alone?

(Diego starts crying. Francois and Natalie both hug him.)

DIEGO

Yes, all my family were taken up with the Rapture. I was as hardcore in my unbelief. I guess I got it from my military background. We were trained to be tough and not easily give in. Now it has hit me hard at the core of my heart.

(Diego starts crying uncontrollably again. Natalie and Francois hold his hands.)

NATALIE

I guess we all are in this. Both me and Francois have been left behind by our families that were taken up.

DIEGO

It's so sad.

FRANCOIS

Yes, Diego, it is, but at the end of the tunnel, there is light. We should be happy to see the real True Light. Soon we will be united with the families that went before us.

DIEGO

That gives me so much hope. Can you please pray with me? I want to give my life to Christ.

FRANCOIS

Of course. That's why we are here, just for you.

(They all pray together, and Diego gives his life to Christ.)

Next scene

(Jean Claude and his family are with Rania at the Tigris River in Baghdad. They are talking about the book of Daniel.)

JEAN CLAUDE

You see, this was where the prophet Daniel received his visions from the Lord.
It was an important revelation he got for this time we are in now.

RANIA

Can you please tell us about it?

JEAN CLAUDE

Sure, he mentioned in the Book of Daniel Chapter 12 verse 11 that from the time that the daily sacrifice is taken away, and the abomination of desolation is set up, there shall be one thousand two hundred and ninety days.

RANIA

What happens after that?

JEAN CLAUDE

After that is the return of Christ with His Bride.

ABIGAIL

Wow, so we don't have much time left?

JEAN CLAUDE

No, we haven't. According to the prophecy, just about 10 days.

ALI

Wow!! What do we do next?

JEAN CLAUDE

I am sure the Lord will let us know soon.
(They drive back to Rania's home.)

Next scene

(Hennie and Ingrid are with Romy in the school hall with all the school kids.)

HENNIE

Romy, I think the first thing we need to do is get all the children together and let us pray with them.

ROMY

That's a brilliant idea.

(Hennie, Romy and Ingrid are praying, standing with the children in a big circle holding hands together. Afterwards, they pray for each child's Salvation in Christ.)

HENNIE

Isn't it strange that your school is next to a church?

ROMY

Yes, apparently, this Church was chosen to receive some relics of Saint Andrew, the first disciple of Jesus, in honour of the ministry that he did here in the time of the first Church.

HENNIE

Wow, that is so interesting. You know the place we are going to take the children to in France is next to the Palace of Versailles. Our good friend Jean Claude has a mansion there. We are a group of people that have met in Paris, and we are all Christians now. Jesus appeared to Jean Claude and told him to call the group "The Last Call". We are doing the finishing work of Christ before He returns with His Bride.

ROMY

That's so amazing. It gives me goosebumps to hear all this.

Next Scene

(Fire shots go off in the city. A large statue of Jesus is still standing in the town of Saidnaya, Syria. It is titled "I Have Come to Save the World." It's the tallest statue of Jesus Christ in the Middle East. Jordan and Katia are hiding in the Church in Damascus with Maria and her friends and family. They pray for the city and rescue people from the street, and bring them into the Church.)

KATIA

There are firing shots everywhere. Let's see if we can help some people in the street and bring them to safety in the Church.

JORDAN

Ok, let's go.

(Jordan and Katia go outside in "Straight Street" and try to rescue people from the street and bring them into the Church for safety. Maria is praying in the Church with her friends and family for the people of Damascus.)

Next scene

(Francois is talking with Diego about Che Guevara. Diego is suggesting to take him and Natalie to the town of La Higuera, where Che Guevara was killed.)

FRANCOIS

It's interesting, Diego, you don't live far from the town where Che Guevara was killed.

DIEGO

No, I don't. I can take you and Natalie to the place today.

FRANCOIS

That will be great.

(Diego is driving with Francois and Natalie to the town of La Higuera.)

Next scene

(It's the morning, and Jean Claude is talking in the living room to his family and Rania about the day.)

JEAN CLAUDE

I feel we should drive to the town of Yusufiyah and go to the Euphrates River. It's only a 20 min drive from here.

ABIGAIL

Ok, let's do it.

(They drive to the Euphrates River at the town of Yusufiyah. They stand next to the Euphrates River.)

JEAN CLAUDE

You know this was the Euphrates River which John the apostle was referring to in the book of Revelation.

RANIA

What did he say about it?

JEAN CLAUDE

I will read it to you. (*Jean goes on his phone.)* It says in Revelation 16:12,

"Then the sixth angel poured out his bowl on the great river the Euphrates, and its water was dried up so that the way of the kings from the East might be prepared."

ABIGAIL

So, this speaks of what will soon happen?

JEAN CLAUDE

Yeah, the armies of the East, which refers to China and their allies of surrounding countries, will come through the Euphrates to go to a place called Armageddon in Israel.

RANIA

Is that the final Battle of Armageddon that everyone is talking about?

JEAN CLAUDE

Yeah. (*Jean goes on his phone and reads to them Revelation 16:16.)* "And they gathered them together to the place called in Hebrew, Armageddon."

Next scene

(Hennie explains to Romy that they need to get ready for their trip back to France.)

HENNIE

Romy, I see you have a lot of kids here that are from Russia, Ukraine and Belarus originally.

ROMY

Yeah, hence the orthodox churches here in our country.

HENNIE

I see. Well, I am so happy we came here, but I have a feeling we should get ready for our trip to France. Jean Claude might call me at any time, and then we should fly back.

ROMY

Ok, I understand. Let me speak to the children and prepare for our trip.

HENNIE

Great.

Next scene

(Katia and Maria are praying together. Katia informs Maria that she needs to leave with Jordan soon.)

KATIA

Maria, it was such a blessing to come here. I am so thankful that God has sent me here with my new husband to help my own people in the most distressing time of all time.

MARIA

We are also so blessed that you came.

KATIA

You know, it all makes sense to me now the vision I had when I was in the Notre Dame Cathedral in Paris. I saw the blood coming out of Maria's eyes. That blood was for the Salvation of the people. I fulfilled my destiny here.

MARIA

Thanks again for coming here. We will be forever grateful. We will see you again when our Saviour comes.
(Maria is hugging Katia.)

Next scene

(Francois, Natalie and Diego are at the building in La Higuera where Che Guevara was shot.)

(The song plays "Hasta Siempre" by Natalie Cardone.)

(A woman called Eva is opening the door of the building to let them in.)

DIEGO

Many thanks, Eva. I will only be a few minutes.

EVA

You are welcome, Diego.

(Diego shows Francois and Natalie the spot where Che Guevara was shot.)

DIEGO

This is the spot where Che was shot. (*They are pondering for a moment.)*
I have brought many people here before, but I have never seen what I see now.

FRANCOIS

What do you see, Diego?

DIEGO

I see that we can be part of a great fight and wars on earth, but if we don't have the King of Kings in our hearts, the fight is in vain. We have to be in the right army. The King of Heaven's army.

FRANCOIS

You are so right, Diego. (*They all give each other a hug.)*

EVA

I assume you all are Christians?

DIEGO

That's true, Eva. These fine people came all the way from France to save me.

EVA

Can you also pray for me? I also want to be a Christian.

FRANCOIS

Of course. Let us pray.

(They pray for Eva, and she gives her life to Christ.)

NATALIE

Eva, we are all going back to France as we have a safe place there before Jesus comes back. You are welcome to join us.

EVA

(Tears go down Eva's face.)

I would love too.

They all give her a group hug.

Next Scene

(Jean Claude is sleeping and then woken up by Jesus.)

JESUS

Jean Claude My beloved servant, it's time to go back. It's time for the final count down. I want you to contact the rest of the group to return to France. I am about to release My 7 angels with 7 golden bowls filled with the wrath of God. This will be My last warning to mankind. I want to show mercy to people out there that respond to My cry in this last hour, then the time is ready for Me and My Bride to come down and destroy the works of the Anti-Christ and his armies…

(Jean Claude wakes up and shares his dream with Abigail.)

(The song plays "The Final Countdown" by Europe.)

JEAN CLAUDE

Abigail, I woke up in the middle of the night. Jesus again appeared to me.

ABIGAIL

Wow. What did He say?

JEAN CLAUDE

He told me that we should go back to France and that I needed to let the others know to return too. He is going to release His 7 angels who will pour down His wrath on earth before He returns with His Bride.

ABIGAIL

That sounds serious. How are the people going to wake up to His warnings?

JEAN CLAUDE

Well, they have to forget about their pride and be humble.

ABIGAIL

It reminds me of our Jasmine.

JEAN CLAUDE

What do you mean?

ABIGAIL

I have read this morning in the bible "Matthew 18:4."

JEAN CLAUDE

What does it say?

ABIGAIL

It says, "Therefore whoever humbles himself as this little child is the greatest in the kingdom of heaven."

(Jean Claude and Abigail go to the living room. They speak with Rania and tell her to go with them to France for safety.)

JEAN CLAUDE

Rania, we have to leave soon to get back to France, but we want you to come with us.

ABIGAIL

Yes, it is for your own safety. Jean had a visitation from Jesus last night.

RANIA

Wow! What did He say?

JEAN CLAUDE

He said He is about to release His 7 angels with 7 golden bowls to pour out the wrath of God on earth. Baghdad will not be a safe place at this time; hence we want you to come with us.

RANIA

I understand. I will get ready.

Next Scenes

(Jean Claude phones the others. ***.*** *The group are flying back from their missions.* ***The song plays "Up where we belong" by Joe Cocker and Jennifer Warnes.***

(Diego and Eva are in the superjet with Francois and Natalie. Rania is also in a superjet with Jean Claude and family.)

(Hennie, Ingrid, Romy and the school kids are flying back to France. Jordan and Katia are teleported back to Jean Claude's mansion.)

(They all gather at Jean Claude's place. There is a grand tent outside Jean's mansion to accommodate the people. The children are playing at the back of the field.)

Next Scene

(The group meet for the last time at Jean Claude's house. They read Daniel 7:27 and Daniel 12:11-12 together.)

JEAN CLAUDE

Well, guys, it's so great to have you all here. Well done; we have fulfilled our separate missions. I think this will be the last time we will have a gathering before His coming. I want to read 2 scriptures out of the Book of Daniel to you, which sum up the time ahead for us, humanity. The first is Daniel 7:27. Which says:

"Then the kingdom and dominion,
And the greatness of the kingdoms under the whole heaven,
Shall be given to the people, the saints of the Most High.
His kingdom *is* an everlasting kingdom,
And all dominions shall serve and obey Him."

FRANCOIS

So, that refers to Jesus's Millennium reign on earth, right?

JEAN CLAUDE

That's right. That's what we have done with our separate missions to prepare the people for His reign on earth. So, we are now coming to the End where Jesus will release His 7 Angels to pour out the bowls of Judgement before His coming for the Final Battle at Armageddon.

HENNIE

So, how will this all play out?

JEAN CLAUDE

That's exactly why I want to read you "Daniel 12:11-12."

NATALIE

Please read it for us.

JEAN CLAUDE

Ok. It says, "[11]And from the time that the daily sacrifice is taken away, and the abomination of desolation is set up, there shall be one thousand two hundred and ninety days.[12]Blessed is he who waits and comes to the one thousand three hundred and thirty-five days."

NATALIE

So, what is happening after the 1335 days?

JEAN CLAUDE

It's the Hanukkah feast, Natalie. The Greatest Feast ever!

Next Scene

(The start of the Bowl of Judgements. The 7 Angels are released.

The temple in heaven appears, and out of it comes seven angels having the seven plagues, clothed in pure bright linen, and having their chests girded with golden bands. One of the four living creatures in heaven gives to the seven angels seven golden bowls full of the wrath of God. The temple is filled with smoke from the glory of God and from His power, and no one is able to enter the temple till the seven plagues of the seven angels are completed.

A loud voice comes from the temple saying to the seven angels, "Go and pour out the bowls of the wrath of God on the earth."

The first angel went and poured out his bowl upon the earth, and a foul and loathsome sore came upon the people who took the mark of the beast and those who worshipped his image.

The second angel pours out his bowl into the sea, and it becomes blood like that of a dead man, and every living creature in the sea dies.

The third angel pours out his bowl on the rivers and springs of water, and they become blood. The angel is saying:

"You are righteous, O Lord,
The One who is and who was and who is to be,
Because You have judged these things.
For they have shed the blood of saints and prophets,
And You have given them blood to drink.
For it is their just due."

The fourth angel pours out his bowl on the sun, and power is given to him to scorch men with fire. People are scorched with great heat, and they blasphemed the name of God, who has power over these plagues, and they do not repent and give Him glory.

The fifth angel pours out his bowl on the throne of the beast, and his kingdom becomes full of darkness, and its people gnaw their tongues because of the pain. They blaspheme the God of heaven because of their pains and their sores, and they do not repent of their deeds.

The sixth angel pours out his bowl on the great river, the Euphrates, and its water dries up so that the way of the kings from the East might be prepared. And I saw three unclean spirits like frogs coming out of the mouth of the dragon, out of the mouth of the beast, and out of the mouth of the false prophet. For they are spirits of demons, performing signs, which go out to the kings of the earth and of the whole world, to gather them to the battle of that great day of God Almighty.

They gathered together to go to the place called in Hebrew Armageddon.)

Next Scene

(THE TAXI DRIVER RICH from the first movie, "The 4 Horses", is driving to La Guardia Airport in his taxi to get a flight to Jerusalem. He has a Scottish flag and an Israeli flag in his Taxi. Next to him sits his Scottish wife, Margaret. ***The song plays on the radio, "You win again", by the Bee Gees.)***

RICH

You know Margaret, you see these Armies from the East. China and all their buddies in crime are going to try and fight the "King of Kings".
They are off their head. That's a fact; I tell you, they are completely mad. That's an insane fact.

MARGARET

Aye. (Translation Scottish: "yes")

RICH

I'll tell you another fact. You know your William Wallace that fought the English on Stirling Bridge?

MARGARET

Of course, our Braveheart hero. How can I forget him?

RICH

Well, that will be the same outcome as that battle on Stirling Bridge. Jesus will wipe them and the Anti-Christ out; now that's a fact. You see, Jesus was born on the 11th of September and that Stirling Bridge event took place on the 11th of September.

There is only one winner there, I tell you that. You know, another fact is that, you know, that Marco Polo guy that discovered China on the Silk road, I tell you he was on his way to China when William Wallace was born in 1270. Now for real, that's a fact.

MARGARET

Richie boy, I am so glad we chose Jesus eventually. Now we are on the greatest winning side of all time!

RICH

I tell you, we were born winners. Your name came from the greatest princess Scotland has ever produced, Saint Margaret. That my beauty is a fact for sure.

MARGARET

So, what are we going to do when we land in Israel?

RICH

Well, we are going to see the greatest fireworks display ever. That's for sure a fact.

MARGARET

What do you mean?

RICH

I mean, by the time we land in Tel Aviv, I am sure "The King of Kings" is coming to meet us in Jerusalem. I am not a prophet, but I tell you a fact, we will just be in time for His arrival with the other saints. Do you remember that couple I told you about that I picked up years back in New York and took to the same airport we are going to now?
They were on their way to Rome. I tell you, that was a golden couple. I am sure we are going to see them with Jesus in Jerusalem. That is 110% fact.

(Rich leaves his taxi outside the front of the airport doors, and he and his wife are running inside the airport to get a flight to Jerusalem on Saints 888 Airline.)

Next Scene

(The seventh angel poured out his bowl into the air, and a loud voice came out of the temple of heaven from the throne, saying, "It is done!" There is thundering and lightning, and a great earthquake happens, such a mighty and great earthquake as had not occurred since men were on the earth. The great city of Rome divides into three parts, and the cities of the nations are falling down.

Every island fades away, and mountains cannot be found. Great hail from heaven fell upon the unbelievers. They are blaspheming God because of the plague of the hail, since the plague is exceedingly great.)

Next Scene

The song plays "We Will Ride", by Lindell Cooley.)

(Lightning and thunder are everywhere in the sky. The sky lights up and opens up. It's all bright. Then suddenly, Jesus appears with His Bride on white horses coming down from the sky.

Jesus is sitting on a white horse. He is called "Faithful and True", and in righteousness, He judges and makes war. His eyes are like a flame of fire, and on His head are many crowns. He is clothed with a robe dipped in blood, and His name is called The Word of God. The armies in heaven, clothed in fine linen, white and clean, followed Him on white horses. Then out of His mouth grows a sharp sword, that with it He should strike the nations. He Himself will rule them with a rod of iron. He has on His robe and on His thigh a name written:

KING OF KINGS AND LORD OF LORDS.

Light illuminates Jerusalem. Jesus goes on the Mount of Olives, and He says, "I am the Resurrection". Graves open on the site of Mount Olives. Jesus opens the doors of the Golden Gate on the east side of the old city walls of Jerusalem, and His Bride follows Him. They move to a place called Armageddon to fight the Anti-Christ and His Armies.

An angel is standing in the sun; and he cried with a loud voice, saying to all the birds that fly in the midst of heaven, "Come and gather together for the supper of the great God, that you may eat the flesh of kings, the flesh of captains, the flesh of mighty men, the flesh of horses and of those who sit on them, and the flesh of the unbelievers, both small and great."

The beast, the kings of the earth, and their armies all gathered together to make war against Him who sat on the white horse and against His army.

Then the beast, who is the antichrist, is captured, and with him the false prophet who worked signs in his presence, by which he deceived those who received the mark of the beast and those who worshipped his image.

The two of them are cast alive into the lake of fire burning with brimstone. The rest are killed with the sword, which proceeded from the mouth of Him, who sits on the horse. And all the birds are filled with their flesh.

The wording comes up: "The kingdoms of this world have become kingdoms of our Lord Jesus Christ.")

Next Scene

(Jesus and His bride are all over the area in the Middle East. The buildings are all in ruins. Jesus talks to His Bride with a loud voice, "It's time to rebuild, like in the time of the prophet Nehemiah. They all gather together for the rebuilding process and start the work everywhere and in Jerusalem.)

(Wording flashes up: "Psalm 127:1 'Unless the Lord builds the house,
they labour in vain who build it")

Next Scene

(It is 44 days later. A Fish barbeque with Jesus at the sea of Tiberias. Millions of people sit on the hills and fields while Jesus explains to the crowd the fulfilment of the 153 fish of John 21.)

JESUS

It's time to rest and for a "Babette's Feast" before the Real Feast is coming. Thanks for all your labouring with Me. Paul, could you remind us again of what you have written in 1 Corinthians 3:9.

(Paul the Apostle is coming to the forefront. Jesus is giving Paul a hug.)

PAUL THE APOSTLE

Sure, Lord. Well, it says, "For we are God's fellow workers, you are in God's field and God's building."

(Scene of millions of people sitting on the fields listening to Christ.)

JESUS

That's correct. Peter said it beautifully in his letters in the Word that you are living stones, being built up into a spiritual house. Peter, can you and John come forward and tell the people how it happened that day when you and the disciples caught 153 fish.

(Saint Peter and John are coming out of the crowd. Peter and John are giving Jesus a hug. A scene of a view on the Sea of Tiberius.)

PETER THE APOSTLE

Well, it was very close to the spot where the scene took place. We were trying to catch fish the previous night but to no avail.
Then, the next morning we tried again. Then we heard a voice from the shore shouting to us to let our nets down on the right side. As we did, we caught an abundance of fish. At first, we didn't know who was standing on the shore, but then John realised that it was Jesus.

JOHN THE APOSTLE

Yes, I recognised His voice.

JESUS

That was always John's strength. He knew My Voice, because he always listened attentively to Me while I was speaking. That's why I could entrust him with the last book in the Bible, the Book of Revelation.
David, can you please come forward.

(King David comes toward Jesus and gives Jesus a kiss on his right cheek.)

DAVID

I guess, Lord, you want me to tell the people about Psalm 110, right?

(Jesus is smiling.)

JESUS

What makes you think like that, David?

DAVID

Well, you said to Peter to throw the nets to the right side, right?

(They both are smiling.)

JESUS

That's right, David.

DAVID

Well, I was writing that Psalm because we were fighting a battle against our enemies, and I cried out to You for help. I heard You say, "Sit at My right hand till I make your enemies your footstool."

JESUS

Yes, that is the very reason why I told the disciples to throw the net to the right side. So, Peter did. I gave Peter the keys of the Kingdom realm to preach the Kingdom of God on the day of Pentecost. So, I used him as a firelighter to start the fire that went to the 4 corners of the world.

David, just keep standing here. I want to illustrate something. Jacob and Benjamin, can you two please come forward?

(Jacob and Benjamin move to Jesus. They both hug Him.)

Jacob tell us why did you name your youngest son Benjamin?

JACOB

Well, Lord, he was born in Rachel's pain, and before she died, she called him Ben-Oni, son of the mourning, but I wanted to change it to Benjamin, meaning son of my right hand.

JESUS

Precisely that was the right thing to do as the tribe of Benjamin was destined to inherit the area of Jerusalem and the New Jerusalem that is prepared for My Bride.

That's also why I gave you that dream of the ladder that stretched to heaven and the angels going up and down from heaven to earth. The new Jerusalem will be coming from above when all things are made new by Me after My 1000-year reign on earth.

THE CROWD OF PEOPLE

Hallelujah!! Blessed be Your name, King of Kings, that will rule for all eternity. Praise to the Father.

JESUS

So, Jacob, that stone that you lay your head on when I gave you the dream, the Stone of Destiny, its weight is, for a reason, 153 kg. That was why Peter and the disciples caught 153 fish. It was to reach all nations that will come to Me.

THE CROWD OF PEOPLE

Glory to the King of Kings! Salvation belongs to You, oh Lord!!!!

JESUS

Benjamin, come stand on the right side of David.

BENJAMIN

Sure, Lord.

(They all stand next to each other. They are facing the crowd, Benjamin on the left, David in the middle and Jesus on the right. Jesus explains to the crowd why they all three were born in Bethlehem.)

JESUS

In My Word, it states that in the mouth of two or three witnesses, every word shall be established. Thus, to establish the importance of Bethlehem, all 3 of us had to be born there.

It's called "House of Bread" for a reason. I am the "Bread of Life". Benjamin had to be born in Bethlehem, because His tribe was allocated the Temple, which is the New Jerusalem. He was a sign pointing to Me as the Second Temple. David had to be born there as through him I established the kingly line of Judah. Micah if you can come forward and tell us about Micah 5:2-5 when you wrote it.

(Micah comes out of the crowd, and he gives Jesus a hug.)

MICAH

Well, Lord, I am honoured that you would want to share the revelation of the verses which I wrote. It was in a time before the destruction of Samaria and Jerusalem. I was a prophet with Isaiah in the land of Judah.

JESUS

I will call out Isaiah next but first, tell us about that beautiful verse you wrote. *(Jesus is smiling.)*

MICAH

Sure, Lord. Well, I think you wanted to give us comfort in the midst of the serious warning of the destruction of Jerusalem in the Land of Judah. You promised that out of a small insignificant town called Bethlehem, the Messiah will be born, who will ultimately lead us all into a time of peace.

JESUS

(Jesus taps Micah on his shoulder.)

That's correct, Micah. That is what this time is about. We will have a 1000-year reign of peace before a final judgment by Father God. Then we will have a new Jerusalem and new earth as it's the finishing of the 7000 years since Adam and Eve, and we will enter the eternal 8th Day for all eternity.

MICAH

I get it now, Lord; that's why Bethlehem is 8km distance from Jerusalem. It's because you were born in Bethlehem to restore the garden of Eden in Jerusalem. You are making all things new.

JESUS

(Jesus kisses Micah on the forehead.)

That's right, Micah. I am making all things new, and it's a new beginning for mankind. Now let's call your old friend Isaiah to the forefront. Isaiah, please come to us.

(Isaiah is coming to Jesus. He gives Jesus and Micah a hug.)

ISAIAH

Thank you, Lord, for calling me forward.

JESUS

(Jesus is smiling.)

Of course, Isaiah. How could I not call you to the forefront? You are the one that wrote a mini Bible before the Bible was completed.

ISAIAH

Lord, you are talking about the 66 chapters of my book?

JESUS

Yes, Isaiah. Like the 66 books of the complete Bible. Your first 39 chapters were about My law representing the Old Covenant, and the next 27 chapters were about My Grace representing the New Covenant.

ISAIAH

Yes, Lord, you gave me foresight about the future.

JESUS

That was your calling. You also prophesied My birth like Micah. Can you tell us what you have written in Isaiah 7:14?

ISAIAH

Of course, Lord. I wrote, "Therefore the Lord Himself will give you a sign: Behold, the virgin shall conceive and bear a Son, and shall call His name Immanuel."

JESUS

That's right. Immanuel means "God with us", and that was what God the Father did with Me, to dwell among His sons and daughters. So, God the Father chose Mary as a chosen vessel to bring Me forth. Let me call forth Mary, the highly favoured one among women, chosen to bring forth the Light of the world.

(Jesus calls forth his mother, Mary. They hug each other. She stands next to him, and Jesus puts His arm around her while He talks about 24 Kislev.)

(The Song plays "Oh Holy Night" By Mariah Carey.)

JESUS

As you know, today is the 24th of Kislev on the Jewish Calendar. On this day, I was conceived. It was all prophesied by Haggai about 500 years before Mary was conceived. She was also conceived on the 24th of Kislev, and she was a chosen vessel by Father God to birth The Messiah.
The date was chosen because it is the day before the start of the Hanukkah Feast, also called the Feast of Lights. The Feast of Lights lasted for 8 days because of the miracle of the oil that lasted 8 days. I have come to fulfil the Feast as I am the Light of the World. Haggai, can you please come forward and tell us about what you have written in Haggai 2:18-19.

(Haggai, the prophet, is walking towards Jesus and gives Him a hug.)

HAGGAI

Well, Lord, it was on the 24th of Kislev, the year 520 BC, that I heard You say, "Consider the day that the foundation stone of the temple was laid. You said, "Is the seed still in the barn?" and that from that day, You will bless Your people.

JESUS

That's correct, Haggai. I was referring to the second temple's foundation stone that was laid, but also to My own conception. I had to come as a perfect Second Adam to rectify Adam's disobedience in the Garden of Eden and to reconcile the World to God the Father on the Cross. Adam and Eve, can you two please come forward.

(Adam and Eve are coming out of the crowd. They hug Jesus.

Jesus is looking at the crowd. He then speaks to them.)

JESUS

I am sure you were all waiting for the story of Adam and Eve from their own mouths.

(The crowd is getting excited. There is a great level of noise.)

JESUS

Mary, can you please go and stand next to Eve, the mother of mankind. I will stand next to Adam.

MARY

Yes, of course, Lord.

(Mary is standing next to Eve while Jesus is next to Adam. Jesus is speaking to the crowd.))

JESUS

This is something I have been waiting to do for 6000 years! (*Jesus smiles.)*

So, with the four of us, Father God illustrated His Love to mankind by sacrificing His only Son so that many can be saved, as it is written in John 3:16 " For God so loved the world that He gave His only begotten Son, that whoever believes in Him should not perish but have everlasting life."

With Adam and Eve, Father God started the human race, and through their disobedience, He brought in the plan of Salvation.

THE CROWD OF PEOPLE

Blessed be the Father! Blessed be the Son, the Saviour of the world!

(The Song plays "There is a river" by Catherine Mullins.)

JESUS

After this 1000-year reign, a new Eden will be created, and within it, a pure river proceeding from the throne of God and of Me.
On either side of the river will be the tree of life, which will bare twelve fruits, each tree yielding its fruit every month.
Adam, didn't I explain this to you after you and Eve have transgressed in the Garden of Eden?

ADAM

Yes, Lord. You said in Your Mercy, after 5 and a half great days, you will restore everything. I only understood it correctly when I was taken into heaven that you have meant 5500 years after the Flood.

JESUS

That's correct, Adam. I have chosen Noah, the tenth generation after you, to build an Ark and start over with him and his family. He was upright among his generation, but none of his generation would listen to him. He warned them about the Flood that would come, but they laughed at him. He and his family were 8 people together. That was again a sign from Me to point to the Eternal 8th Day that would come after the 7000 years are completed. Noah, can you please come forward?

(Noah is coming out of the crowd. He greets Jesus and gives Him a hug.)

JESUS

Noah tells the crowd a bit about your life on the Ark and that first day you and your family got out of the Ark.

NOAH

Well, that Ark was our safe haven. We felt that You were looking after us every day and protecting us from the whole Flood that came on the earth. We were so glad when the waters went down and when the dove that we had sent out returned with an olive leaf. We knew the time had come.

JESUS

On that note, let me call Ron Wyatt. He was given a special task to show My evidence of great events that have taken place in the Bible. He was My Indiana Jones of the previous generation before the last generation at My Second Coming. Ron, could you please come forward.

(Ron Wyatt is coming out from the crowd. He gives Jesus a hug.)

JESUS

Ron, come and stand next to Noah here and tell us about that discovery of the remains of Noah's Ark.

(Ron stands next to Noah.)

RON WYATT

Well, Lord, I was looking at an article in Life Magazine about a boat-like shape on a mountain near Mount Ararat. The possibility that this could be the remains of Noah's boat put me on a career path as an amateur archaeologist.

JESUS

Well, Ron, as I have so many times shown through the generations, I don't choose people for their credentials but for who they are and what I have created them to be. I could trust you with so many findings. That's why I could give you the ultimate finding of My Ark of the Covenant. It made you My real Indiana Jones. *(Jesus smiling.)*

RON WYATT

I am forever grateful for that Lord.

JESUS

That discovery of the Ark of the covenant in Zedekiah's Cave underneath Golgotha, where I was crucified, was crucial because that led to your most important finding after that. Before we go into that, let Me call Jeremiah the prophet to the forefront. Jeremiah, would you please come forward.

(Jeremiah comes to Jesus and gives him a hug.)

JESUS

Jeremiah, tell us exactly what happened with the real Ark of the Covenant.

JEREMIAH

Well, Lord, it was King Nebuchadnezzar II that captured Jerusalem and took King Zedekiah, the last king of Israel, to Babylon. You have instructed me to hide some holy treasures with the Ark of Covenant in the Cave of Zedekiah.

JESUS

That's true. I have done that for the very purpose of knowing that I would have to die on the Cross on Golgotha for the Salvation of mankind. The Ark of Covenant was just in the Cave at the spot below My Cross. Ron, could you tell us what you saw in the Cave when you saw the Ark of Covenant.

(Tears are running down Ron's face.)

RON

Lord, I saw Your blood stains on a crack in a rock that dripped on the Ark of the Covenant. I was a nurse anaesthetist by trade, so I could take blood samples to the lab in Tel Aviv to do an analysis.

JESUS

What did it show Ron?

RON

Lord, it showed only 24 Chromosomes instead of 46. The one extra chromosome has never been seen before.

JESUS

That's correct. The 23 chromosomes came from Mary, and the extra 1 Y chromosome came from Father God. So, when I was on the Cross, there was an earthquake and the rocks rent. The Roman soldier next to Me put a spear into my stomach. Blood was coming out, and it went through the rocks and sprinkled unto the Mercy seat of the Ark of Covenant, which was 40ft below the Cross. Let Me call Abraham and Isaac to explain something. Abraham and Isaac, please come to Me.

(Abraham and Isaac are coming to Jesus. Jesus hugs both of them.)

JESUS

Abraham, can you please tell us about that 3 day's journey with Isaac to Mount Moriah.

ABRAHAM

Of course, Lord. You told me to go to the region of Moriah and to sacrifice my only son, Isaac, at the age of 37 as a burnt offering on a mountain that You would show me.

JESUS

Did you tell Isaac that?

ABRAHAM

No Lord. I only told him right at the point where I needed to put him on the altar.

JESUS

Isaac, how did that make you feel?

ISAAC

Well, Lord, it made me very scared, but I felt I needed to obey my father. There must be an explanation for why he would do that.

JESUS

Of course. That's exactly how I felt before I went to the Cross. So, what happened then, Abraham?

ABRAHAM

Just as I was about to do it, an angel stopped me. A lamb was provided in Isaac's place.

JESUS

Correct. That lamb was symbolic of Me that would one day die on a cross for the Salvation of mankind. That was Father God's plan of Salvation, and you, Abraham, were chosen to be a type of Father God who would be willing to sacrifice his only son because you had faith in Me that I would provide. That's why I have called you for a reason, the father of all nations. You were the 10th seed after Noah. You were a sign to the people of Father God and your son Isaac a sign of Me, as the Son God. I gave you the gift of hospitality so that you can communicate well with all types of people, regardless of their background or ethnic group. Soon we are going to do a barbeque, and I want you to light the fire.

ABRAHAM

It will be my pleasure, Lord.

JESUS

First, I want Daniel to come here before we start the fire. Daniel, can you please come forward and tell the people about Daniel 7:27 and Daniel 12:11-12.

(Daniel comes forward and gives Jesus a hug.)

JESUS

Daniel, tell us about that favourite scripture, Daniel 7:27.

DANIEL

Well, Lord, that scripture I wrote in the first year of king Belshazzar's reign.

JESUS

That's right. Remind us again what it says.

DANIEL

It says," Then the Kingdom and dominion, and the greatness of the kingdoms under the whole heaven, shall be given to the people, the saints of the Most High. His Kingdom is an everlasting kingdom, and all dominions shall serve and obey Him." It looks like that scripture is getting fulfilled right now. (*Daniel smiles.)*

(Jesus smiles. He puts both of his hands on each shoulder of Daniel and looks into his eyes.)

JESUS

You are correct, Daniel. I tell you another scripture of yours that is also right now being fulfilled is Daniel 12:11-12. Tell us about it.

DANIEL

Well, I saw in the first year of the reign of Darius the Mede that vision. I saw You Lord in white linen above the waters and the two angels asking you what the end shall be like?

JESUS

What did I say?

DANIEL

You said, "And from the time that the daily sacrifice is taken away, and the abomination of desolation is set up, there shall be one thousand two hundred and ninety days. **12** Blessed *is* he who waits and comes to the one thousand three hundred and thirty-five days."

JESUS

Amen. Jesus looks at the crowd and says in a loud voice, "Be blessed, children of God." Let's enjoy today our fish barbeque because tomorrow night we will celebrate the Greatest Feast, The Hanukkah Feast.

(Jesus walks to the barbeque area with Abraham. As they reach the area, Jesus hands Abraham a firelighter to start the fire. Abraham lights the fire. A view of all the abundance of the fish ready to be grilled.)

Next Scene

(The First Day of the Feast of Hanukkah in Jerusalem starts. It's the 30th of November, St. Andrews Day.)

(Jesus welcomes His Bride. He steps through a door where it is written on top of it, " The Doorway of Favour, Isaiah 62:4." St. Andrew and Neil Armstrong are standing next to Jesus. Neil Armstrong has his Scottish kilt on. Jesus speaks to all the saints.)

JESUS

Welcome, My beloved! You have entered into the favour of God. You are Mine, and I am yours forever. As it is St. Andrews Day, let Andrew open up for us with a few words about the Feast of Feasts.

ANDREW

Well, thanks, Lord! It's such a privilege to open this Feast. I feel I am on the St. Andrews golf course, having the first swing at the ball. (*The crowd laughs out loud.)*

Well, I am a man of few words; my brother Peter is the big talker.

(St. Andrew is smiling.)

All I can say is I am so glad that I took that first step to follow Christ. In the words of Neil Armstrong, "That's one small step for man. One giant leap for mankind."

(St. Andrew is putting his arm around Neil Armstrong. Neil Armstrong is smiling.)

Next Scene

(Jodhi and Helen are talking with the taxi driver Rich and Margaret at the Hanukkah Feast.)

RICH

Jodhi and Helen. I tell you a fact. Today on Saint Andrew's Day, we are celebrating the first day of the Hanukkah Feast. Didn't I tell you back in the day that things would work out for both of you?!

JODHI

You did, and that's a fact. (*All three of them are laughing.)*

HELEN

So nice to see you here, Rich. I remember so clearly when Jodhi and I met you. It was so funny, we were laughing all the way in the taxi to the airport.

RICH

Yeah, it was so great to meet you guys. I told Margaret I couldn't wait to see you guys here! If it wasn't for Margaret, I probably wouldn't have come to my senses and received Jesus as My Saviour.

(*Ernst and Emma are joining them together with David Livingstone.)*

JODHI

Oh, hello, Ernst and Emma.

ERNST

Hello Jodhi. I have bumped into a fellow you really want to meet. (*Ernst is smiling.)*

Meet David Livingstone. (*Ernst introduces David Livingstone to the group.)*

(Rich shakes his hand)

RICH

Oh wow! Dr Livingstone, I presume. (*They all are laughing.)*

JODHI

It’s so nice to meet you finally. You are one of my heroes. Not only because we share the same surname. (*Jodhi is smiling.)*

DAVID LIVINGSTONE

Well, Jodhi, you were one of my heroes. You took the baton from me. You finished the race that I have started.

JODHI

That’s so kind of you to say that.

DAVID LIVINGSTONE

Yeah, I really mean it.

JODHI

Thanks, brother. (*They give each other a hug.)*

ERNST

I am so glad, David, that I have found you in the crowd. I knew I should take you to Jodhi. He always talked about you. (*Ernst is smiling.)*

DAVID LIVINGSTONE

Well, I am so glad I have met you guys. Let me introduce you to John Hanning Speke, the founder of Lake Victoria. He is just standing there.

(David Livingstone is waving at John Hanning Speke.)

(Jodhi, Ernst and David Livingstone are walking to John Hanning Speke and David Livingstone introduces him to Jodhi and Ernst.)

JOHN HANNING SPEKE

Wow, David, so nice to see you again.

DAVID LIVINGSTONE

Yeah, same here. I have two fine men I want to introduce to you. Meet Ernst and Jodhi. They both were born in South Africa.

JOHN HANNING SPEKE

It's such a privilege to meet you guys.

(They all shake hands.)

JOHN HANNING SPEKE

I know you two played a pivotal role in the great tribulation. I was part of the cloud of witnesses who were watching it from heaven's arena.

JODHI

Thank you, but you laid out the map for us. You found the northern border for the place prepared for God's remnant in the Great Tribulation.

JOHN HANNING SPEKE

Well, God has been kind to me to be able to go on that mission to find the source of the Nile.

(Jodhi sees in the corner of his eye Anita, who was the secretary in San Francisco when he went for an interview. He winks at her and calls her to the group.)

JODHI

Oh, so nice to see you here. I have never forgotten that interview in San Francisco.
It was such an important stage in my life. That's the time I met Helen.

ANITA

So nice to meet you again, Jodhi. It seems things worked out very well for you.

JODHI

Yeah, thanks to God. Let me introduce you to the people here. This is my lifelong friend Ernst. He is also from South Africa.

ANITA

So nice to meet you, Ernst. (*They shake hands.)*

JODHI

And this is David Livingstone and John Hanning Speke. (*They all shake hands.)*

ANITA

So nice to meet you both. You are big legends. There is one thing I have in common with you, John.

JOHN HANNING SPEKE

REINHARD

I get it. (*They all are having a laugh.)*

Next Scenes

(Thomas, the disciple, is talking to a few people from India. He is telling them about his landing there and also about the girdle he caught of Mary at her assumption in Jerusalem. Vasco da Gama is joining the group with Adam Smith. Adam Smith explains, "The invisible hand of God". Marco Polo is joining the group too. Mother Teresa, Mary, the mother of Jesus and Mary Magdalene with her sister Martha are also there.
Christopher Columbus and Bartolomeu Dias join the group.)

THOMAS, THE DISCIPLE OF JESUS

It was the 21st of November AD 52. I was landing at Cochin, India. It was my mission to spread the gospel to India.

VASCO DA GAMA

Well, Thomas, I followed in your footsteps. I was the first European to find an ocean trading route to India. I landed on the 20th of May, 1498, at Calicut and died at Cochin on Christmas Eve. We also spread the gospel of Christ to India.

CHRISTOPHER COLUMBUS

Interesting point. I was on a mission to go to the opposite way than you to reach India.
Instead, we discovered the Americas, but it happened to be that I died on the 20th of May, 1506. Exactly eight years after you reached India.

VASCO DA GAMA

I remember that. It was big news in the world of exploration the day you died.
It's great to see Bartolomeu Dias here. He was a great inspiration to me in finding the route to India. He was a visionary ahead of his time.

BARTOLOMEU DIAS

Well, you two guys did a great job. I am glad that I could pave the way for you guys.

MOTHER TERESA

And you guys have paved the way for me. Although I was from Albania, my mission was to take care of the poor in India and reach them with the love of Jesus. I remember the day I decided to be a missionary. It was on the 15th of August, 1928, and I was at the shrine of the Black Madonna of Vitina-Letnicë.

MARY, MOTHER OF JESUS

That was the date of my Assumption.

MOTHER THERESA

Yes. I was very aware of that.

THOMAS, THE DISCIPLE OF JESUS

How could I forget that day? I was there.

MARY, MOTHER OF JESUS

Thomas, maybe it is a good time to tell them the story.

THOMAS, THE DISCIPLE OF JESUS

Ok, that's a good idea. As you know, I kind of got a reputation among Christians to be called "Doubting Thomas". I was not with the gathering of the other disciples on the evening of Jesus's Resurrection day. So, I disbelieved the disciples when they said they had seen Christ.

MARY MAGDALENE

Well, Thomas, you don't have to feel that bad. I saw Christ first on the morning of His Resurrection, and I told the disciples that I had seen the Lord. They also doubted me.

MARY, MOTHER OF JESUS

But then Thomas the Lord was gracious to you. You were the only one of the disciples to see my Assumption.

THOMAS, THE DISCIPLE OF JESUS

That's correct, Mary.

Next Scene

(Joshua and Caleb are talking to Christian, the son of Jodhi, about their lives.)

JOSHUA

Caleb, back in those days when we were fighting for our Promised Land, we didn't know how good this day would be.

CALEB

Absolutely, we were just happy that we could have our own land and territory.

CHRISTIAN SON OF JODHI

Hello. My name is Christian, and my third name is Caleb. My father liked the name Caleb from the Bible. It's so nice to meet you two. You are legends in the Bible.

CALEB

Well, it is such an honour to meet you, Christian. You got the correct first name because you indeed were a follower of Christ in your day.

CHRISTIAN, SON OF JODHI

Thank you. Could you please tell me about the battle of Jericho?

CALEB

I let Joshua start as he was our true leader back in the day.

JOSHUA

Well, we were facing great giants in our day. We were so dependent upon God.
He taught us for 40 years how to trust in Him while we were in the wilderness.

CALEB

God trained us in the wilderness to become good leaders so that one day we could take the next generation to victory in the Promised Land.

JOSHUA

So, in the battle of Jericho, we had to listen to God to win the victory.
Jesus appeared to me, and he gave me the strategy of how to take Jericho.

CALEB

Yes, the strategy Joshua gave us in the natural didn't make any sense, but then the outcome was superb. So, it taught us a lesson.

CHRISTIAN

What did it teach you?

CALEB

That we must not reason things out in our head, but just obey Him when He gives us instruction.

JOSHUA

Yes, and that's how we won the battle.

(King David and Jesse, the father of King David, join the conversation.)

KING DAVID

I heard a bit of the conversation. I think one thing we have all learned back in those days was that the battle is the Lord's and the victory ours.

CALEB

David would know. He was Israel's hero in the fight against Goliath. I am proud to be also from the tribe of Judah, just like David is, but we still love everyone from the other tribes! *(Caleb smiles.)*

JESSE, KING DAVID'S FATHER

And I am very proud that David is my son. *(Jesse smiles.)*

(Jessica, the sister of Christian, is joining the conversation.)

CHRISTIAN

This is my sister Jessica.

JESSE, KING DAVID'S FATHER

You are beautiful, Jessica. Your name sounds like my name.

JESSICA, DAUGHTER OF JODHI

Thank you. Well, my name is from Jesse in the Bible.

JESSE, KING DAVID'S FATHER

I am Jesse in the Bible. (*Jesse is smiling at Jessica.)*

JESSICA

Wow, that is so cool. Where is King David?

JESSE

This is him standing next to me.

(Jessica is blushing.)

KING DAVID

Nice to meet you, Jessica. (*David is smiling at Jessica and shaking her hand.)*

JESSICA

Can you please tell me the story of how you slew the Giant?

KING DAVID

Of course, I get asked that question all the time from all age groups.

JESSICA

I am so excited to hear the real story from you.

DAVID

Well, I was in the field looking after our sheep. My father called me and asked if I could take some food for my brothers to the battlefield. I was excited because I wanted to see the battle. When I got there, Goliath was standing on his own, screaming with a loud voice at the army of the Israelites. He was mocking them. I thought this couldn't be; who does he think he is. Goliath was requesting a champion from Israel's army to fight him, but no one wanted to come forward as Goliath was a massive Giant.

JESSICA

How did it happen that you fought him?

DAVID

I knew King Saul because sometimes I went to play music for him. I noticed he was on the battlefield, and I went to ask him if I could fight Goliath. In the beginning, he was a bit resistant, but then he let me do it.

JESSICA

How come you were not scared to fight him?

DAVID

Well, I first knew that God was on my side and that He would give me victory.
Secondly, when I was looking after the sheep, I had to protect the sheep from wild animals. I struck down a bear and a lion with my sling slot and killed them. I thought I could easily do the same with Goliath. As the saying goes, the rest is history.
(David is smiling.)

JESSICA

Wow, that is such a great story!

KING DAVID

Thank you, Jessica.

Next Scene

(It's a scene back to Reinhard Bonnke talking to Martin Luther and the group of Reformers. They are talking about The Reformers Wall in Switzerland.)

MARTIN LUTHER

Reinhardt, as you have met John Calvin, let me introduce you to the other three of the Reformers Wall.

REINHARD BONNKE

Sure.

MARTIN

Meet William Farel, a friend of John Calvin. He was the founder of the Calvinist Church in Geneva. He persuaded John Calvin to stay in Geneva. It became the "Rome" of the Protestant movement.

REINHARD BONNKE

So nice to meet you.

WILLIAM FAREL

My pleasure. You were a great Evangelist in Africa. You spread the good news everywhere you went.

REINHARD BONNKE

Thank you. It was my passion for Christ.

(Theodore Beza is standing next to John Knox. Martin Luther introduces them to each other.)

MARTIN LUTHER

This is Theodore Beza. He was a disciple of John Calvin and succeeded Calvin as the spiritual leader of the Republic of Geneva.

REINHARD BONNKE

A pleasure to meet you, Theodore. (*They shake hands.)*

THEODORE BEZA

Good to meet you too, Reinhard.

MARTIN LUTHER

And then the last, but not the least. This is, of course, John Knox, the last of the four men together on the Reformers Wall.

REINHARD BONNKE

So nice to meet you, John Knox. I know everything about you.

JOHN KNOX

You do? (*John Knox smiles. They shake hands.)*

REINHARD BONNKE

Obviously not, but you were kind of a great influencer. I researched a lot about you and the impact you had in Scotland. You started the Church of Scotland.

JOHN KNOX

Thanks. Indeed. Caledonia. (*John Knox smiles.)*

(The Song plays "Caledonia" by Dougie MacLean.)

MARTIN LUTHER

Finally, meet the famous Sculptor Paul Landowski.

REINHARD BONNKE

It's a privilege to meet you, Mr Landowski! (*They shake hands*.)

MARTIN LUTHER

Mr Landowski was a very talented sculptor. He not only helped with the Reformation Wall but also did the famous statue "Christ the Redeemer" in Rio de Janeiro.

PAUL LANDOWSKI

Thanks for all the compliments, but I was truly only inspired by the real Creator, Jesus Christ Himself.

(Bartolomeu Dias is joining the group.)

BARTOLOMEU DIAS

Excuse me for eavesdropping, but I heard you say Mr Landowski did the "Christ the Redeemer" statue in Rio.

MARTIN LUTHER

That's correct, Bartolomeu! Gentlemen, meet the great explorer Bartolomeu Dias.

He was the first European to round the Cape of Good Hope. I was only 4 years old at the time, but I remembered what my dad told me. It was probably the first thing I remembered from my childhood! It was indeed very big news in the age of discovery!

BARTOLOMEU DIAS

That's very kind of you to say that, Martin, but I can't help overhearing the conversation you had with Mr Landowski. We also planted a cross in Mossel Bay, South Africa, in 1488 to point to Christ our Redeemer. Actually, on one of my last voyages, a strong wind took us to Brazil, and that's how we discovered Brazil, God's destiny for us.

(Martin Luther notices Billy Graham is standing nearby talking to Smith Wigglesworth and Emily Hobhouse. He invites them to join their conversation.)

MARTIN

What an interesting group you are.

BILLY GRAHAM

Thanks. It's just an honour for me to speak to these fine British people. Let me introduce them to you.

(Billy Graham is introducing Smith Wigglesworth and Emily Hobhouse to the group.)

EMILY HOBHOUSE

Please to meet you all. Billy Graham and I were just discussing with Smith Wigglesworth his prophecy of the last revival on earth before Jesus Second coming.

BILLY GRAHAM

Yeah, what is very fascinating is that not long after that prophecy in 1947, I started my first crusade in the same year.

SMITH WIGGLESWORTH

That's correct. I prophesied my last vision shortly before I died.

MARTIN

Could you please share that vision with us? (*Reinhard Bonnke is also listening attentively.)*

SMITH WIGGLESWORTH

Of course. I remember clearly what I said.

I said: During the next few decades, there will be two distinct moves of the Holy Spirit across the church in Great Britain. The first move will affect every church that is open to receiving it and will be characterised by the restoration of the baptism and gifts of the Holy Spirit.

The second move of the Holy Spirit will result in people leaving historic churches and planting new churches. During the duration of each of these moves, the people who are involved will say, 'This is a great revival.' But the Lord says, 'No, neither is this the great revival, but both are steps towards it.'

When the new church phase is on the wane, there will be evidence in the churches of something that has not been seen before: a coming together of those with an emphasis on the Word and those with an emphasis on the Spirit.

When the Word and the Spirit come together, there will be the biggest move of the Holy Spirit that the nations and the world have ever seen.
It will mark the beginning of a revival that will eclipse anything that has been witnessed within these shores.

The outpouring of God's Spirit will flow over from the United Kingdom to mainland Europe and, from there, will begin a missionary move to the ends of the earth.

REINHARD BONNKE

Yeah, that was a profound prophecy for the last generation! Shortly after Billy Graham and I were taken from the earth, God started the awakening of his soldiers for the last battle. Let me introduce you to this couple. They have experienced the last wave.

(Reinhard is pointing to Ernst, Emma and Saint Martin of Tours. He calls them to join the group. They are standing with the group.)

REINHARD

Ernst and Emma tell us about that last move of God. We saw it from heaven, but you guys experienced it on earth.

ERNST

Well, it was amazing! It was like God opening up the gates of heaven and pouring down His fulness.

EMMA

We saw healings everywhere, and everyone who came with sickness was healed! It was like experiencing Jesus's own ministry of 2000 years back when He was on earth.

ERNST

Emily, it is so nice to finally meet you. *(Ernst shakes Emily's hand.)*

I was always a great admirer of you. Although you are of English origin, you helped the South African people in a great hour of need in the Second Boer War.

EMILY

That's kind of you to say that, Ernst.

ERNST

It's so great to see you and Smith Wigglesworth together. Do you know what you two have in common?

EMILY

Yes, I know we are both British. (*Emily smiles).*

ERNST

(Ernst smiles too.)

No, no. Smith Wigglesworth was born on the 8th of June 1859, the year before you were born, but you were taken by the Lord on the 8th of June 1926, the same year Queen Elizabeth was born.

EMILY

That's fascinating. She was a great Queen! She was only a small baby when I went to heaven, but I met her in heaven after her long reign on earth.

ERNST

Yeah, I saw her in 2005 when she was on the Island of Guernsey. I used to live in St.Martins, Guernsey. Funny I was just chatting with Saint Martin after whom the parish in Guernsey was named. Everybody meet Saint Martin of Tours.

They are all smiling and shaking his hand.

MARTIN LUTHER

Wow, I always wanted to meet the Saint after who I was named. I was baptised on your feast date the 11th of November.

SAINT MARTIN

Well its such a privlige to meet you. You did tremendous work in the Body of Christ. I always wanted to meet you but I guess Jesus kept the moment for the right time at this Great Feast.

MARTIN LUTHER

Amen brother.

Next Scene

(Joseph, the son of Jacob, is talking with Adam Smith about his book the "Wealth of Nations." Adam Smith introduces Andrew Lloyd Weber to Joseph. They talk about the "Joseph Amazing Technicolour Dreamcoat" show.)

JOSEPH

It's great to talk to you finally, Adam Smith. We were both used in our times to pioneer the wealth of nations. (*Joseph shakes Adam Smith's hand.)*

ADAM SMITH, SCOTTISH ECONOMIST

Very true. Well, Joseph, it's my privilege to meet you! Your story has inspired every household in the world. I want you to meet my fellow Brit, the great composer Andrew Lloyd Weber. He made your story famous throughout the world with his musical comedy in theatres, called "Joseph the Amazing Technicolour Dreamcoat."

JOSEPH

I am very aware of that show. (*Joseph is smiling. He shakes Andrew Lloyd Weber's hand.)*

(Jacob, Ephraim, Manasseh and Joseph of Arimathea join the group.)

JACOB

Sorry for interrupting, but I was in that show too. (*Jacob is smiling.)*

JOSEPH

(Joseph smiles and gives Jacob a hug.)

I know you like that show; that must have got your attention when we were talking about it.

JACOB

Indeed!

JOSEPH

Thanks for bringing my two sons too! (*Joseph gives Ephraim and Manasseh a hug.)*

JACOB

Remember, they are mine too! (*Jacob is smiling.)*

JOSEPH

I remember. You laid your hands upon them and gave each one of them a blessing before you died.

JACOB

That's correct. Can you tell us what I said?

JOSEPH

Sure. I brought both of them beside your knees and bowed down with my face to the earth. And I took them both, Ephraim with his right hand towards your left hand, and Manasseh with his left hand towards your right hand, and brought them near you.

Then you stretched out your right hand and laid it on Ephraim's head, who *was* the younger, and your left hand on Manasseh's head, guiding his hands knowingly, for
Manasseh *was* the firstborn. And you blessed me and said:
"God, before whom my father's Abraham and Isaac walked,
The God who has fed me all my life long to this day, The Angel who has redeemed me from all evil, Bless the lads; Let my name be named upon them,

And the name of my father, Abraham and Isaac;
And let them grow into a multitude in the midst of the earth."

When I saw that you laid your right hand on the head of Ephraim, it displeased me; so I took hold of your hand to remove it from Ephraim's head to Manasseh's head. And I said to you, "Not so, for this one is the firstborn; put your right hand on his head."

But you refused and said, "I know, my son, I know. He also shall become a people, and he also shall be great, but truly his younger brother shall be greater than he, and his descendants shall become a multitude of nations."

So, you blessed them that day, saying, "By you Israel will bless, saying, 'May God make you as Ephraim and as Manasseh!' " And thus, you set Ephraim before Manasseh.

(Joseph of Arimathea, the uncle of Jesus, joins the group. He introduces Herbert Armstrong.)

JOSEPH OF ARIMATHEA

Hello, my friends. Do you mind me joining the conversation? I have someone I want to introduce to you.

JOSEPH, SON OF JACOB

Of course, it's our privilege. People meet Joseph of Arimathea, our Lord's uncle. I guess he has a lot of stories to tell us. (*Joseph, son of Jacob, is smiling.)*

JOSEPH OF ARIMATHEA

You are right, Joseph; that's why I brought my friend Herbert Armstrong along.
We have a lot in common, especially my feast date, which is the 31st of July, and he was born on the 31st of July. It was his destiny to continue the story I started when I visited Britain for the first time with Jesus as a little teenage boy after his father Joseph died.
(Joseph of Arimathea introduces Herbert Armstrong, and they all shake his hands.)

JOSEPH, SON OF JACOB

Joseph, could you please tell us more about the story of you and Jesus going to Britain?

JOSEPH OF ARIMATHEA

Of course. It will be my privilege. We landed in Britain with my boat on the shores of Cornwall. I was a trader in metal. We traded with England in copper and tin. I brought Jesus with me as his father just died recently before that.

Then 5 years after Jesus's ascension to heaven, I again came with many disciples in AD 37 to Britain. There was a great persecution against the Christians in Israel at that time, so I came permanently to settle down in Britain.

The staff that I have planted in Glastonbury can still be seen until this day. It grew into a mighty tree.

JOSEPH, SON OF JACOB

So, you came to Britain permanently in AD37 and exactly 2000 years after that, in AD 2037, the Great Tribulation started all over the world.

JOSEPH OF ARIMATHEA

That's correct, Joseph. Well observed.

(John Smith is joining the group with Pocahontas and John Rolfe. He tells the story of the first landing of the English at Jamestown, USA.)

JOSEPH, SON OF JACOB

Wait, here comes John Smith with John Rolfe and Pocahontas. It just got even more interesting.

JOHN SMITH

Hello, my good friend Joseph. Look at my two friends whom I brought with me.

JOSEPH, SON OF JACOB

You couldn't come at a better time. We were just discussing Joseph of Arimathea's permanent settlement in Britain. I bet the group would love to hear from all 3 of you the story of the First English Settlement in Jamestown, USA.

JOHN SMITH

Well, I guess you have the right people here to tell you that story.
(John Smith is smiling.)
I was not only there with the Jamestown settlement in 1607 but also helped with the map for the Plymouth Settlers.

I went to that area in 1614 and named it New England. Then six years later, the 1620 Settlers established a colony there at Plymouth, USA.

JOSEPH, SON OF JACOB

That's brilliant, but tell us about that famous landing at Jamestown. I am sure everyone here wants to hear that story. *(Joseph is smiling.)*

JOHN SMITH

Well, we arrived on the 13th of May at Jamestown, and the whole crew settled down on the 14th of May. It was a 144-day journey from England with 144 crewmen.

JOSEPH, SON OF JACOB

It sounds like The Book of Revelation, where the number 144,000 is pivotal.
(Joseph is smiling.)

JOHN SMITH

Almost. It was also the 14th of May, the future date of independence for Israel in 1948. We felt somehow at the time that we were part of a special mission.

HERBERT ARMSTRONG

It is so interesting to hear this story from the real people that we have read about in books. I can't help but interrupt as it was a very important statement that you have made, John Smith.

JOHN SMITH

About the 14th of May?

HERBERT ARMSTRONG

Yes, indeed. We listened to the prophecy of Jacob over Ephraim and Manasseh before. Well, it was at this time that God was starting to bring the prophecy to fulfilment. Remember Jacob said let my name Israel be on both of you.

JOSEPH OF ARIMATHEA

Could you please explain to us, Herbert?

HERBERT ARMSTRONG

Of course. It was in 1603 that King James VI became king over England, Scotland and Ireland. It was with the First English Settlement in North America that the separation of birthright between Ephraim and Manasseh would take place.

JACOB

That's correct, Herbert! That what I have prophesied over the young lads was coming into fulfilment.

HERBERT ARMSTRONG

Yes, Jacob, Ephraim, which represents Britain, would become Great Britain in 1801, a powerful company of nations after Manasseh, who represents the USA, who would get its independence in 1776. So, Ephraim would become the Commonwealth of Nations and the USA a great nation.

ADAM SMITH

Yes, so that's when I published my book "The Wealth of Nations" on the 9th of March, 1776.

JOSEPH, SON OF JACOB

Yes, it was on the 4th of July 1776 that the 13 Colonies in the USA got their independence.

HERBERT ARMSTRONG

Remember Jacob said let my name Israel be on both of you.

JOSEPH, SON OF JACOB

Yes, he did.

HERBERT ARMSTRONG

So, God established Israel in North America to become a great nation there. It grew from one colony to thirteen and then to 50 states.

JOSEPH, SON OF JACOB

That's correct. Fifty stands for Salvation. My story end in the book of Genesis with chapter 50, which is the last chapter in the Book of Genesis. So, John Smith, tell us what happened after your landing on the 14th of May?

JOHN SMITH

Well, at midnight on the 14th of May, we got attacked by the Native Indians.

HERBERT ARMSTRONG

It sounds familiar. When Israel gained their independence on the 14th of May 1948, it got attacked from Palestine the very next day. I remember it clearly as I founded The Ambassador College a year before in 1947.

JOSEPH OF ARIMATHEA

Yes, we always need to let our minds stay focused on God. He is faithful to protect us and bring us into His victory.

JOSEPH, SON OF JACOB

Indeed. So, John, then you met Pocahontas after your landing? *(Joseph smiles.)*

JOHN SMITH

Not yet, Joseph. (*John smiles.)*

It was only at the end of that year, in December, when I was exploring the area, that I was captured by the Native Indians. They took me to Chief Opechancanough, who was actually the brother of Pocahontas's father, Chief Powhatan. I was made a spectacle before several of the native tribes before I was actually taken to Pocahontas's father. I was kept under their rule for a few months.

One day they were placing my head on two stones, and a warrior was ready to kill me. However, Pocahontas intervened that day by placing her head on mine to stop him. It was a very brave thing to do for an eleven-year-old girl. I let her tell her version of the story.

(John Smith is looking at Pocahontas.)

POCAHONTAS

Well, I was still a very young child, but my father loved me so much that he listened to me. It didn't feel right that they would kill John Smith. That was when I put my head upon his head. They eventually released him to go back to his people. I went there from time to time to give them some food, but I eventually got married to one of our tribe leaders.
I hadn't seen John Smith for years before I came to London. I was so shocked to see him there as I was told before that he was killed.

JOSEPH, SON OF JACOB

So, you were by then married to John Rolfe?

POCAHONTAS

Yes.

JOSEPH, SON OF JACOB

So, tell us the love story. Everyone is waiting for that. (*Everyone is smiling.)*

POCAHONTAS

Well, let me give John Rolfe a chance. I am sure he will be good at it.
(Pocahontas is smiling at John Rolfe.)

JOHN ROLFE

Well, Pocahontas was captured by the English. We had our English settlement in Henricho. We taught her our ways and about Christianity; hence she was given a new name, Rebecca. I got to know her, and we fell in love. We got married in Jamestown on the 5th of April, 1614. She was only 17 years old at the time.

JOSEPH OF ARIMATHEA

So, what made you go to London?

JOHN ROLFE

The Virginia Company wanted Pocahontas to meet the Royal Family for good relations between the Native Indians of the Americas and Britain, plus to show the success of the Virginia colony. It worked well, but unfortunately, Pocahontas fell ill on her journey back to Virginia. We only sailed back as far as Gravesend in England, where she eventually died on the 21st of March, 1617.

Next Scene

(Helen is talking to Saint Margaret of Scotland and her son, King David I of Scotland.)

HELEN

It's such a privilege to meet you, Margaret. Jodhi told me so much about you as he was also half Scottish and was interested in your history.

SAINT MARGARET

Thanks. It's an honour to hear your story, as you two did great things in your time!

HELEN

Oh, thank you.

SAINT MARGARET

Please, meet my son David.

HELEN

So nice to meet you, David. (*They shake hands.)*

DAVID, SON OF SAINT MARGARET

It's my privilege.

HELEN

So, Margaret, could you please tell me the story of how you ended up in Scotland? I know it from the history books, but it's so much better to hear it from a real person itself.

SAINT MARGARET

I was born in Hungary and was the daughter of England's Prince Edward, the exile, and my mother was Agatha from Hungary. We were living in Hungary until 1057 when my father was recalled back to England to be the possible successor to my great-uncle, King Edward the Confessor, who was childless. Unfortunately, my father died as we were landing in England. We remained to stay in England as my brother Edgar was a possible successor to the English throne.

This was the time of the Norman invasion of England, and my mother thought we should go back to Hungary. My mother wanted to protect me, and we were fleeing away to Hungary. We first fled to Northumbria, England, and then we took a boat and sailed to Europe, but a storm led us to Scotland. As you would know yourself, it was never planned that way, but events led to it.

Thus, I met King Malcolm III. We fell in love and got married. It was my destiny to come to Scotland, and God was good to us, or should I say God was gracious to us.

(Saint Margaret smiles.)

HELEN

Yes, Gracious sounds right to me. If it wasn't for God's grace on us, we wouldn't be able to accomplish the things we did on earth.

SAINT MARGARET

Correct, my dear. *(Margaret gives Helen a hug).*

(Jeremiah with Tea Tephi arrives on the Scene and greets Helen, Saint Margaret and David, son of Margaret.)

JEREMIAH, THE PROPHET

My oh my, what an interesting group of people.

SAINT MARGARET

Always nice to talk to you, Jeremiah. You have done such important work coming to Britain in your time.

JEREMIAH

Well, I was sent to Britain on a secret mission by the King of Kings to establish His throne on earth there. Please meet princess Tea Telphi, the daughter of the last king of Judah, King Zedekiah.

TEA TELPHI

I feel honoured to be in the midst of such great people of God.

SAINT MARGARET

It's great to meet you, Tea. I feel we are all only great servants of the One who is truly Great.

TEA TELPHI

That's correct.

HELEN

We are very much looking forward to hearing your full story and especially how you came to Britain.

SAINT MARGARET

We are very intrigued by that story. So, tell us everything.

(Everyone is excited to hear Tea Tephi's story.)

TEA TEPHI

Well, it is my privilege to tell it. Although it was a heartbroken time for me as my father, King Zedekiah, was captured by King Nebuchadnezzar of Babylon and my brothers were killed in front of his eyes. I was taken care of by Jeremiah. We were travelling with the Stone of Destiny via Egypt and via the Straits of Gibraltar, then Breogan, Spain, where we stayed for a while.

After Spain, we left for Ireland, but we were blown in a storm up north for several days. We sighted land and entered the bay at Mara-Zion, near St. Michael mountain in Cornwall.

At Mara-Zion, we met Elatha, the powerful ruler of Cornwall. He welcomed us in a very friendly manner and swiftly had our boat repaired. He then sent a message to the High King of Ireland to notify him that I was coming and requested a guarantee of safe passage for me.

JEREMIAH

Sorry for interrupting, but another important point I want to highlight is that we told Elath about the fall of Jerusalem. He wept bitterly, and that's why the name of that place in Cornwall is called 'Mara-Zion', which means in Hebrew "Bitter for Jerusalem".

You may carry on Tea. (*Jeremiah is smiling at Tea.)*

TEA TEPHI

That's ok, Jeremiah. (*Tea is tapping Jeremiah on the shoulder.)*

So, I received a message of welcome from Ireland with a lot of silver and gold as a gift to show that I would be safe. King Eochaidh sent his family's most treasured heirloom, a piece of jewellery which is called the "Sun of Helen of Troy ".

(Brutus, the founder of London, arrives on the scene.)

BRUTUS

Hello, my name is Brutus; when I heard you talk about Helen of Troy, it captured my attention.

(They all greed Brutus. Eli and Samuel also arrive at the Scene.)

SAMUEL

Can we also join? It looks like an interesting conversation here?

JEREMIAH

Sure, my good friend Samuel. Tea Tephi is just telling our story of how we landed up in Ireland.

SAMUEL

Please continue your story, Tea.

TEA TEPHI

Well, I was talking about the piece of jewellery called the "Sun of Helen of Troy" which King Eochaidh sent me while I was in Spain. Apparently, his forefathers had won it as a spoil of war at the Battle of Troy, where his Zarahite ancestors and the Danite greek ancestors of the Irish people, including Ulysses, had built their famous Trojan horse, that had successfully fooled the Trojans and gained them access to their city.

BRUTUS

Wow, I know this story very well. The Battle of Troy started after Helen of Troy became Helen of Sparta. Achilles was there, and the famous saying ' The Achilles heel' came from that battle where Achilles died of a wound in his heel. I was a descendant of the Trojan hero Aeneas and the founder of London, which I called the New Troy.

ELI

Yes, I remember it very well. It was in my time. News spread very fast to Canaan about the new city in Britannia.

BRUTUS

Yes, they changed the name later from *Troia Nova* ("New Troy") to Trinovantum. It was after it was rebuilt by King Lud, who named it *Caer Lud* ("Lud's Fort") after himself, and this name became corrupted to *Kaer Llundain*, and finally London.

Next Scene

(Marco Polo and his father are talking with Ernst, Emma and their daughter Mulan.)

MARCO POLO

So, you guys named Mulan after the famous Chinese warrior girl?

ERNST

Yes, I thought it was a great idea, as Emma's mother came from China.

EMMA

Yeah, and it worked out well. She has that type of warrior spirit.

(Mulan is smiling.)

NICCOLO POLO, MARCO POLO'S FATHER

Do you want to know one of the greatest mistakes we have made regarding Christianity in our time?

EMMA

Please tell us.

NICCOLO POLO, MARCO POLO'S FATHER

I was travelling with my brother in 1266 in China. We were meeting Kubla Khan, who wrote to Pope Gregory X to send him 100 men who were skilled in Christianity. Pope Gregory X, who was at that stage unable to see the future, only sent two. At that stage, Khan's territory stretched over one-fifth of the globe's inhabited land.

ERNST

Wow, it's a very interesting point you made.

(William Wallace spot Marco Polo with the group and introduce himself)

WILLIAM WALLACE

Hello, I could not help but hearing your conversation. It's a privilege to meet you finally Marco Polo! I am William Wallace from Scotland. I heard so much about your travels in my time on earth. You started travelling to Asia when I was conceived.

(William Wallace is smiling.)

MARCO POLO

Yeah, you are right! I have heard of you too! You were Scotland's hero when you fought the English at Stirling Bridge. The Real Braveheart infront of my eyes! *(Marco Polo is smiling.)*

ERNST

So nice to meet you William Wallace! I am Ernst. I always took a like in your story. This is Emma and Mulan, our daughter.

WILLIAM WALLACE

The pleasure is mine! Nice to meet all you lovely people.

Next Scene

(Back to the group with Tea Telphi.)

TEA TEPHI

After receiving the positive answer and invitation from Ireland, Elatha sent his son Bressail, who was Nuadh, the king of Ulster's champion and fifty-three ships, with two thousand and five men, to escort me safely to Ireland. So, we ended up in Ireland, which was my destiny to be.

HELEN

When did you arrive in Ireland?

TEA TEPHI

It's better to ask Jeremiah. He is good with dates. (*Tea Tephi is looking at Jeremiah and smiles.)*

JEREMIAH

It was on the 18th of June, 583 BC. We arrived with a ship at the port of Howth, where we were welcomed by Eochaidh, the High King of Ireland. We went to the Hill of Tara on the 20th of June. Tea got married there with Eochaidh. I am sure Tea, you can remember your own wedding date? (*Jeremiah is smiling at Tea Tephi.)*

(Tea Tephi is smiling.)

TEA TEPHI

Of course. It was the 21st of June, the very next day after we reached the Hill of Tara.

(Ezekiel and St. Patrick are joining the group.)

JEREMIAH

Well, well, my old friend and contemporary Ezekiel. (*Jeremiah gives Ezekiel a hug.)*

EZEKIEL

I overheard your conversation, and I felt Patrick and I should join this conversation.

JEREMIAH

Great idea. Nice having you here, Patrick. You and I are so joined to Ireland's history.

SAINT PATRICK

For sure, the Emerald island was our destiny.

JEREMIAH

Speaking about destiny, well done to you guys for looking after the Stone of Destiny.

SAINT PATRICK

Well, we knew it was an important Stone.

JEREMIAH

But I think you are mostly remembered for your story with the Three Leaf Clover.

SAINT PATRICK

Yes, because it has great significance. I could illustrate the Trinity of God with it, but even the 4-leaf clover has a special meaning behind it.

TEA TEPHI

What would that be?

SAINT PATRICK

It speaks about the four gospels, Matthew, Mark, Luke and John, in the New Testament. The gospel of Christ reaches the 4 corners of the world.

EZEKIEL

Yes, it reminds me of the 4 faces I have seen of the Cherubs that God has shown me. The face of a man, a lion, a bull, and an eagle.

JEREMIAH

That's right. Tell us Ezekiel about that scripture you wrote in Ezekiel 21:26.

EZEKIEL

Well, it says:

"Remove the turban, and take off the crown;
Nothing shall remain the same.
Exalt the humble, and humble the exalted."

JEREMIAH

And that was the whole purpose of my mission to Ireland. I had to take Tea Tephi to Ireland to marry a descended from the Zerah line of Judah.

PATRICK

Yes, I spent most of my life in Northern Ireland, and they had symbols of the red hand, which came on the Ulster flag in later years.

JEREMIAH

That's correct. We read in Genesis 38 that Tamar gave birth to twin boys for Judah.

At the time of giving birth, twins were in her womb. When she was giving birth, the one put out his hand; and the midwife took a scarlet thread and bound it on his hand, saying, "This one came out first." It happened, as he drew back his hand that his brother came out unexpectedly, and she asked, "How did you break through? This breach be upon you!" Therefore, his name was called Perez, meaning "Breach". Afterwards, his brother came out, who had the scarlet thread in his hand. And his name was called Zerah.

It was prophesied in Genesis 49 that Judah is like a Lion, and the sceptre will not depart from his lineage. So, the Perez line was the line where the kings of Judah came from, and in Ireland, God was exalting the Zerah line through King Eochaidh marrying Tea from the Perez line.

EZEKIEL

That's amazing how God showed that to me. You were the instrument in His hand to fulfil His purpose.

JEREMIAH

Yes, that's why when we visited Spain, which was called in my time Heberia, we visited the descendants of Zerah. They built the city "Zaragoza", which means Stronghold of Zara.

EZEKIEL

So, God united the two lines, Zerah and Perez.

JEREMIAH

That's correct. The breach that Perez was called after was healed by uniting them.

EZEKIEL

So, after the marriage took place between Tea Tephi and King Eochaidh, what did you do?

JEREMIAH

I stayed in Ireland and died there on the 21st of September. That's why that date became my feast date.

Next Scene

(Ruth and her husband Boaz are talking with Jodhi and Helen. Esther and Mordecai join the conversation.)

RUTH

Jodhi and Helen, let me introduce you to Esther, a great woman of faith.

HELEN

So nice to meet you, Esther! Your story has inspired so many women to take action in their walk of faith.

ESTHER

Thanks, Helen, but I knew God had placed me in a position to help my kinsmen. Mordecai told me if I remained silent and did not take the risk to act on behalf of them, then God would do it through someone else, and my family and I would perish. So, I obeyed.

MORDECAI

Yes, and it's because of Esther's obedience that God released her kinsman back to Jerusalem, and she was greatly blessed.

ESTHER

I must say I was inspired as a young child by the story of Ruth. Your marriage to Boaz had a lot of hidden meanings.

RUTH

Well, at that time, I didn't know the whole meaning, but I was aware that God's hand was upon Boaz and me.

HELEN

Yes, Jodhi and I were discussing the 6 jars of water that Jesus turned into the finest wine with his first miracle at the wedding feast. It reminded me of the 6 measures of barley that you brought to Naomi out of the harvest field just before Boaz, and you got married.

RUTH

Yes, correct. It symbolised the 6000 years until Jesus's Millennial reign on earth as the King of Kings. Boaz was my redeemer, just as Jesus is all of us Redeemer.

BOAZ, HUSBAND OF RUTH

I was honoured to be Ruth's redeemer. She was not only a beautiful woman but had a great quality about her.

RUTH

Aww, thanks, Boaz. *(Ruth gives Boaz a hug.)*

(St Francis, Clare of Assisi and St Lawrence are joining the group. Everyone is greeting them.)

HELEN

Francis is such a privilege to meet you. You mean a lot to Jodhi and me. We met in San Francisco, and our destiny's collided. We know San Francisco is named after you.

SAINT FRANCIS

Well, thanks, that's so good to hear.

Saint Lawrence and I were just discussing how he was entrusted, during a period of great Christian persecution in His time, with the Cup of Jesus of the Last Supper. The Cup eventually ended up in Valencia, Spain.

JODHI

That must have been a very important assignment. That cup represents the price He has paid on the Cross for us. It was buckets of blood that were spilt for the remission of our sins.

SAINT LAWRENCE

That's correct. The price He has paid for us was enormous.

SAINT FRANCIS

Jodhi and Helen, please meet Clare of Assisi. She was one of my first followers. A great woman of God.

HELEN

I have read a lot about you and St. Francis. Both of you inspired Jodhi and me.

CLARE OF ASSISI

That's very kind of you to say. Thanks to both of you two for what you have done in God's kingdom.

JODHI AND HELEN

Thank you, Clare. *(Jodhi and Helen gives Clare a hug.)*

Next Scene

(Ernst and William Wallace are talking about the Star of South Africa diamond that launched the diamond industry in South Africa.)

ERNST

You know what is interesting is that my great grandfather lived as a child on that Zandfontein farm near the Orange River, where they discovered the Star of South Africa diamond, which launched the diamond industry in South Africa and the whole world.

WILLIAM WALLACE

So, when did that happen?

ERNST

It was in 1869.

WILLIAM WALLACE

Do you know what is super interesting? (*William Wallace is smiling.)*

ERNST

No, tell me.

WILLIAM WALLACE

I got to know later that they dedicated that William Wallace monument in Stirling, Scotland, on the 11th of September 1869 to commemorate that victory we had at Stirling Bridge.

ERNST

Wow, same year! We have something in common. (*Ernst is smiling.)*

(Ernst spot Stella from the second movie of the Trilogy, "The Greatest Departure ", and call her to join the conversation.)

ERNST

Hello Stella. Come and join our conversation. Meet the hero of Scotland, William Wallace.

STELLA

Nice to meet you, William. That Braveheart movie during my time on earth really made your story famous all over the world.

WILLIAM WALLACE

I like that movie too! (*William Wallace is smiling.)*

ERNST

Stella is one of my friends. I met her at a barbeque we had in South Africa.

WILLIAM WALLACE

You have a nice name!

STELLA

Thanks. It means star.

WILLIAM WALLACE

I am sure you are a star! (*William Wallace is smiling at Stella.)*

Next Scene

(Solomon speaks with John D. Rockefeller, Eric Liddle and Roger Banister.)

KING SOLOMON

So, John D. Rockefeller, you became even richer than I was on earth.

JOHN D. ROCKEFELLER

Well, The Lord was gracious to me. I asked him for a long life and to make good money. He blessed me beyond what I have asked for. But your life was very inspirational to me. You became king of Israel at the early age of 18.

KING SOLOMON

Yeah, I asked for wisdom at that age, and He gave me everything abundantly and even more.

JOHN D. ROCKEFELLER

Yes, I recognise that 1000 was an important number in your life. All your blessings symbolised that.

KING SOLOMON

That’s correct. It was a pointer to this time of Jesus's Millennial reign on earth as the King of Kings. But these guys have run a great race on earth. Eric and Roger tell us about your running. You were made for speed.

ERIC LIDDLE

Yes, that was His blessing on our lives. We were made for running.

KING SOLOMON

But you also honoured Him.

ERIC LIDDLE

I believed in what the Bible says, that he who honours Me, I will honour too.

KING SOLOMON

And you, Roger, you did what men thought was impossible by running the mile in under four minutes.

ROGER BANISTER

Yes, because I believe what is impossible for man is possible with God.

KING SOLOMON

Well, we have all run our races. Now it is our time to reign with Christ.

(Moses, Elijah and John the Baptist appear on the scene with the 2 witnesses, Boaz and Jachin, standing on each side of Jesus.)

MOSES

Well, you two witnesses have run your races greatly. You were administrators of God's power, just as Elijah and I were in our days. Now you have become great pillars in God's Eternal Kingdom. The keys of the Kingdom belong to Him. All glory to Him!

(All the people around Jesus's throne bow down and give Him glory.)

(Movie ends with a flash of Hennie, Ingrid, Francois, Natalie, Jordan, Katia, Jean Claude, Abigail and Mulan standing together and listen to Jesus speaking to them. Jesus is smiling at them.)

The song "Chariots of Fire" by Vangelis plays.

THE END

SONG LIST:

1) " Higher Love" by Steve Winwood
2) " James Dean" by Bonnie Tyler
3) " Someone to You" by Banners
4) " My Jesus, My Saviour " by Darlene Zschech
5) " I think we're alone now " by Tiffany.
6) " Nothing Gonna Stop us now " by Starship
7) " Marry you " by Bruno Mars
8) " My heart will go on" by Celine Dion
9) " Danger Zone" by Kenny Loggins.
10) " Hasta Siempre" by Natalie Cardone
11) " The Final Countdown" by Europe
12) "Up where we belong" by Joe Cocker and Jennifer Warnes
13) "We Will Ride", by Lindell Cooley
14) " You win again" by the Bee Gees
15) " Oh Holy Night" Mariah Carey
16) " There is a river" by Catherine Mullins
17) " Caledonia" by Dougie MacLean
18) " Chariots of Fire" by Vangelis

Printed in Poland
by Amazon Fulfillment
Poland Sp. z o.o., Wrocław
15 February 2023

2c71072d-bc90-4757-a6d5-3c9623f31e59R01